Deceptions

Also by Rebecca Frayn

One Life

Deceptions

A Novel

REBECCA FRAYN

WASHINGTON SQUARE PRESS
New York London Toronto Sydney

Washington Square Press
A Division of Simon & Schuster, Inc.
1230 Avenue of the Americas
New York, NY 10020

Originally published in Great Britain in 2010 by Simon & Schuster UK Ltd

Manufactured in the United States of America

ISBN 978-1-4391-9639-7

I would like to thank Belinda Allen, Suzanne Baboneau, Lisa Bryer, Annabel Hackney, Andy Harries, Kate Iles, Francesca Main, Jennifer Nadel, Maggie Phillips, Emma Thomas, Charlotte Thompson, and Paul Yule for their invaluable input along the way.

Most of our platitudes notwithstanding, self-deception remains the most difficult deception. The tricks that work on others count for nothing in that very well-lit back alley where one keeps assignations with oneself: no winning smiles will do here, no prettily drawn lists of good intentions.

Joan Didion

Prologue

Ask me why I have never told this story before and I will tell you quite straightforwardly. I've always believed one must strive to put painful episodes behind one with the minimum of fuss and bother. In an age obsessed by introspection I may be out of step, but it's nonetheless a strategy that has served me perfectly well.

Until this morning, when the letter came—one glimpse of that distinctive handwriting enough to conjure her out of the darkness again, tentatively smiling that pearly smile of hers.

More in apprehension than hope, I tore the envelope open. Inside, a birthday card! After all these years of silence, she has sent me a birthday card . . . I suppose the vagaries of the overseas post must have sabotaged its punctual arrival. On the front of the card was a painting by Constable, while inside she had added nothing but her name. It was only as I was about to throw the envelope away that the newspaper cutting fluttered free. Overcome by foreboding, I hastily secreted it in my pocket, where it has remained ever since. I will read it presently. Of course I will. But for the time being, the possibility that our private misfortune could have excited further publicity is more than I can bear.

Once work is over, I drive to the coast in the hope that the sea will soothe me. But the attic door stands ajar now—forbidden memories clamoring and agitating as if in deliberate defiance of my authority. At the time I considered myself a man more sinned against than sinning. Why then does the view backward suggest a rather more sinister interpretation?

26

It happened on a dazzling spring day in April. One that had in every other way been quite unremarkable. Monday mornings were always a hurried affair, the alarm at seven summoning each of us from our beds to make our preparations for the coming day.

In the year since I had moved in with Annie, my attempts to introduce some order into the household had made little impression. As usual, the sink was still stacked with dirty plates from our supper the night before. We had barely embarked on breakfast before the milk ran out, and as we ate there was once again no indication that Dan, Annie's twelve-year-old son, was even yet awake. Several times, with mounting impatience, Annie went to the foot of the stairs and called his name, before hastening back to the kitchen to throw together a packed lunch for his younger sister Rachel and gather coursework for her classes that day. As often happened, certain key papers had been mislaid, prompting a new flurry of panic. Then there were the usual squawks of protest when Rachel's hair had to be brushed and another bout of frantic searching when her school shoes could not be found. I, for my part, sat quietly at work on my BlackBerry while all of this went on, for I had learned by now to allow the daily dramas of the household to flow over me.

And Dan? What of Dan? Afterwards I could at best recall a wraithlike presence who sloped down the stairs at the eleventh hour to stand for some while adjusting his tie and preening his hair in the hall mirror. Annie remembered his cramming schoolbooks into his bag and a last bite of toast into his mouth. She had hovered briefly at the front door to watch as he set off at a half run, mounting his father's old bicycle as he went. Later she was to bitterly regret how distracted she had been. Perhaps she might have borne it all a little better, she said, if she had only thought to bestow a farewell kiss, or an affectionate last word. Instead, she had rather mechanically called after him to *take care on the road*—to which he'd responded with a brief roll of the eyes, before turning the corner and vanishing from our lives.

Once college finished at five, as yet oblivious that anything might be amiss, Annie had collected Rachel from the childminder before stopping off to pick up some food for supper. She had chosen chicken Kiev as a special treat, because she knew it was Dan's favorite dish. It had been a tiring day, and she was fortified by the thought of the large glass of white wine she had promised herself once she got home.

She and Rachel arrived home shortly after six to find the place in darkness. Though Dan usually got back at four, he had recently taken to meeting up with schoolfriends from the sprawling council estate just down the road, and Annie had agreed to these occasional excursions on the strict understanding that he was back no later than six thirty. Assuming his return could only be imminent, a myriad of domestic duties soon distracted her. She put the oven on, poured herself the long anticipated glass of wine, and sat down to peel potatoes while overseeing Rachel's homework. Once that was done she returned a phone call to her sister Emma she had been meaning to make for days, and as she chatted with the phone balanced between shoulder and ear, she simultaneously put in a load of washing.

The moment the conversation ended, noting with a start that six thirty had come and gone, she rang Dan's mobile, more irritated than anxious to find herself being put through to his voice mail. Annie had given in to Dan's pleas for a mobile phone only once he started secondary school and it became apparent it would be the best way to keep tabs on him. But it had proved a far more fallible system than she had anticipated, since he was obliged to switch the phone off while at school and more often than not simply forgot to switch it on again once he left. And so it was, as she later explained to the police, that each little misgiving was readily rationalized and set aside.

* * *

By seven she experienced the first real pang of unease. The sky was rapidly darkening, and his supper now ready. It was cold outside. She couldn't imagine what might be detaining him. She tried his phone again and then, in growing alarm, sought out the class contact list. She rang a few names at random. John wasn't home. Rajesh said they'd spoken at final register. She left a message for Obi, who rang back to say that he had last seen Dan setting off from the school gates at three thirty on his bicycle. He'd definitely been heading home. At least he had presumed he was. Dan certainly hadn't mentioned having plans of any kind. He'd probably just bumped into some friends on the way and lost track of the time. Obi sounded so unperturbed that when Annie put the phone down, she found her apprehension had somewhat subsided again. She even remembered congratulating herself on having resisted the impulse to call me. It was always a matter of pride to Annie not to fuss unnecessarily.

Mentally preparing a sharp lecture for Dan when he stepped through the door, she gave Rachel a bath, read her a story, and put her to bed.

So it wasn't until eight that evening that my phone finally rang at work, and a tremulous-sounding Annie asked if I thought she should call the police. I'm ashamed to recall that I didn't give the question serious consideration, distracted as I was by a document I was preparing. So with my mind only half engaged I offered her the reassurance I presumed she required of me. On the cusp of becoming a teenager, Dan's unreliability was becoming something of a strained joke between us.

"You know what he's like, Annie. Any minute now, he'll swing through that door, the center of his own universe, utterly clueless that his poor mother might be climbing the walls."

"That's just what I thought you'd say," she said, sounding rueful.

At nine exactly, Annie finally called the police. As the minute hand clicked into alignment with the twelve she pressed the first digit of their number, as if an imperceptible displacement of air had triggered her index finger. I arrived home just as a police car was drawing up outside. It was only then that I experienced the first real twinge of foreboding, for its presence struck such a discordant note in that spick-and-span close, with the curtains of the houses drawn and the golden glow of warmth and light within. I waited while they parked, and after brief introductions we walked together down the garden path. I had no sooner unlocked the door and invited them in than Annie flew out of the kitchen, her face falling when she saw it was just the three of us.

Once the officers had taken her statement, more police arrived to search the house and garden in the hope that Dan might be found hiding somewhere nearby. Further rein forcements came to comb the area with tracker dogs, and as the clock drew towards midnight, I set off to walk the meadows and towpath in their wake, standing for some while with deepening apprehension beside the river, before losing heart and turning back. Though I dimly noted the brilliance of the moon overhead and the sweet scent of the flowering horse-chestnut trees that drifted on the night breeze, everything now appeared subtly tainted with menace.

Annie and I took it in turns to walk about the house, to switch the television on then off, frequently glancing towards the clock as it marked the interminable small hours.

"He's been taken," Annie would periodically weep. "*Someone has taken my son*."

When Rachel rose for school, she found us in the living room with two new police officers bent diligently over their notebooks. She stood in her nightdress at the door, surveying the scene in some bewilderment. Though Annie attempted to offer an explanation, her lips only moved wordlessly, and after a moment, Rachel came instead to me and climbed on my lap. I explained as best I could that Dan hadn't come home from school and that the police were here to help us find him, to which she only nodded, asking nothing more as I prepared her breakfast and got her ready for school.

From the sitting room I could hear the low rumble of questions. They were asking if Dan had any enemies, or past episodes of running away. Whether he had appeared anxious or depressed. And to all of these inquiries Annie replied emphatically in the negative. When I took Rachel in to say good-bye, Annie turned to us with unseeing eyes. For a moment I feared she might try to prevent her daughter from leaving, and hastened to reassure her it was for the best—that I would both take and collect her myself. Annie appeared to give this dazed consideration before gesturing her consent.

"It's going to be fine," she said, as much to herself as to Rachel, who was scrutinizing her mother with wide, solemn eyes. Though she was only eight, from the outset the child seemed to grasp the gravity of the situation in a manner that belied her tender years.

By the time I returned, the officers had set off for Fishers Comprehensive to talk to Dan's teachers and classmates and to search the building and grounds, before scouring his route home. Yet no one they spoke to could account for Dan's movements after Obi's last sighting of him at the school gates. Annie became newly distraught at this news when they reported back to us.

"Children don't just disappear into thin air," she protested. "How can no one have seen anything? It doesn't make any sense."

"Well, when you think about it, a thousand odd schoolkids flooding out of the gates at the same time . . ." The officer shrugged. "All of them dressed in the same uniform. Perhaps it's not that surprising."

A new, more meticulous search of the house and surrounding area was made. Annie refused to leave the house, but I went to watch the police as they moved in lines across the meadows, methodically combing the land. Their search had all the logic of a dream in which the incongruous and the inevitable have somehow become one, and I stood looking on, while the hedgerows blazed with their bright new shoots, and the breeze stirred the fallen petals of the cherry trees so festively about their feet.

Then I set off for Fishers Comprehensive to retrace Dan's daily route home for myself. I walked slowly, looking about me carefully, along the leafy street that housed his school and across the busy junction beside the Fishers Estate, before the short stretch of terraced houses that bordered the playing fields and meadows brought me to the modest West London close in which we lived.

The morning passed with the police continually coming and going. Annie sat crouched and mute at the table as if in a state of continual readiness to rush to the door. Occasionally, the sensation of being trapped in a waking nightmare might abate—only for the apprehension to return with a jolt, so vividly renewed it was impossible to know how we could continue to endure it. Yet all the while, ordinary life continued on all about us. Through the window, women in hijabs still passed to and from the estate, pushing buggies, while the high-spirited cries of football games floated now and then from the playing fields beyond. I seem to recall a carpet-cleaning company ringing to offer their services at a cut-price rate and that I only uttered an exclamation of incredulity before replacing the handset without a word. When I switched on the news at lunchtime, it was disconcerting to find that our plight apparently hadn't warranted a single mention among the day's significant events.

A trace on Dan's mobile drew a blank. Further interviews with teachers and classmates failed to throw any new light on matters—no apparent enemies, the police said, no running feuds of any kind. They asked us to cast an eye over a chart in which Dan's name was inscribed at the center of a wheel whose spokes represented every person they had established as being part of his life, whether casual acquaintance, family member, teacher, or friend. Annie kept it beside her and every now and then would turn it over to study it with blank, uncomprehending eyes. Little by little, as word spread, a stream of neighbors and friends began to arrive to keep vigil with us and milled about the kitchen, making tea and conversing in discreet undertones.

By the end of that first day we had been assigned a senior officer who was to head the investigation. Chief Inspector Stanley, I think he was called. If I have trouble recalling his name, I have even greater trouble recalling his face. Perhaps his suitability for the job lay partly in this very invisibility. A gaunt and rather slight man comes to mind, with a complexion so pallid he was evidently accustomed to working long hours in a sunless office. But though you might easily have overlooked him in a crowd, I soon formed an impression of a flinty and precise mind, and came to see that his avoidance of social courtesies indicated no more than an impatience to get quickly to the nub of the matter.

It must be said that in the face of Annie's rather hazy recollections, Stanley's quietly dogged pursuit was frequently taxed to its limits. Annie had a tendency to be imprecise about details, while her response to a direct question could often be puzzingly tangential, and this lifelong tendency was undoubtedly exacerbated by distress. On Stanley's arrival, she began digging through the overflowing drawers of the dresser in search of a recent photograph of Dan, speaking all the while in a breathless rush.

"I had it, just before you came. But I've put it down somewhere and now . . . now it's gone again."

Stanley sat at the kitchen table, his notebook open and the pen poised above the blank white page.

"Julian, you haven't seen it, have you?"

I shook my head and patted the chair beside me, inviting her to join me, but she only closed the drawer slowly, looking about the room with a distracted air.

"Why does everything in this house vanish?"

Then, realizing what she'd said, she put her hand to her mouth with a small *oh*, and finally sat down on the seat beside me.

At once, Stanley cleared his throat and went to work.

"Mrs. Wray, as I understand it from the information you have already given my colleagues, Dan has no history of running away. Nor does he have, so far as you are aware, any involvement with drugs or crime."

"No . . . or rather yes, that's true. He's only just twelve, you see. And still quite young for his age."

"Well, what we need to do now is build up a character profile of Dan. Is he, for example, the rash and impulsive type—a risk-taker—or is he more the shy and retiring kind?"

Annie was nodding as he spoke, her brow puckered in concentration, and she was just turning to consult me, when Stanley cut across her.

"I'd like to begin—if I might, Mr. Poulter—by talking alone with Mrs. Wray."

I rose at once, muttering that I would be upstairs if I were needed. However, Annie's eyes remained downcast on the table, as if she were pondering deeply on his question, and she gave no indication of having heard me.

It wasn't until some while later, when Stanley called my name, that I was shaken from the stupor into which I had fallen. In the kitchen I saw that Annie had evidently been crying again, and she left the room without even glancing in my direction.

"Let's get some of the basics down, shall we?" Stanley turned over a new page in his notebook, smoothing it flat in readiness. "You are an art consultant?"

"Yes. I authenticate paintings."

"And how long is it that you and Mrs. Wray have known one another?"

I made a rapid calculation, somewhat surprised at the answer. "Well, we've lived together for a year now. And we were seeing each other for at least a year before that."

He watched me thoughtfully for a moment. "And how would you describe your relationship with Dan during that period?"

"In the early days of our relationship, things were cordial enough," I said carefully.

"And since moving in?"

"I think it would be fair to say that once Dan realized I was going to become a permanent fixture in his mother's life, our relationship became rather more . . . strained. But while there have undoubtedly been some teething problems, I have always been confident that things would settle down in time."

Stanley nodded. "Mrs. Wray told me you had recently informed him of your wedding plans."

"Yes, that's right. Only last weekend, in fact."

"I would be interested to hear your account of how Dan received this news."

"Not much to say, really. After Annie accepted my proposal, we agreed I should be the one to tell him. She felt it would be better coming from me. Saturday was a beautiful day, so we decided to go for a walk in the park. Dan wasn't keen, but after some resistance he eventually agreed. Then in the café, while Annie and Rachel went off to choose some treats, I . . . I seized the opportunity."

"And?"

"Well. He didn't say very much. But then he never does. He's not a boy of many words."

* * *

The truth was, when Annie had nodded meaningfully at me, before drawing Rachel to the queue for refreshments, I had experienced a momentary touch of . . . what? Pique, I suppose. Surely it used to be the father-in-law whom a prospective suitor was traditionally required to consult? I couldn't but feel a little wrong-footed by this mission now the moment had arrived, unsure of whether I was asking or telling him. Should I assure him of the depth of my love, and the promising nature of my prospects in life? We took the only table still unoccupied, and Dan sat down sideways on the chair so that his face remained averted.

"I have some good news for you," I began. But instead of turning to listen, he bent forward to fiddle with the bindings of his trainers.

"What would you say if I told you that your mother and I had decided to get married?" I pressed on, addressing his left ear. At first he appeared not to have heard me.

"Dan?"

"*What?*" He threw his head briefly in my direction, speaking with the weary exasperation of one who begrudges even the small expenditure of air.

Not wishing to give him the satisfaction of knowing he had succeeded in goading me, I could only repeat the question in as cheery a manner as I could contrive, though he was once again immersed in the minute adjustment of his laces.

* * *

I looked at Stanley, who was watching me with a stony expression, his pen poised over his notebook, and raised my hands in wry exasperation, as if to share with him the frustration of a man caught in such a situation.

"You know what kids are like at that age."

"Well, he may not have said much, but perhaps you could tell me what it was he *did* say?" Stanley asked, after a pause.

"I think he said that it was a free world—that as far as he was concerned, we could 'do what we liked.'"

Stanley nodded. *I see.*

I had still been weighing my response to Dan when Annie rejoined us holding a tray piled high with an assortment of food and drinks. "So! How are we getting on?" she had asked, her anxious smile pivoting between us.

"Dan and I have just been having a nice little tête-à-tête and—"

But the boy had leaped to his feet with an explosive sigh, and though Annie called his name as he pushed past her, the glass doors were already closing behind him. We watched in dismay as he mounted his bicycle and began to hurtle up and down the flagged terrace outside, making skid stops at either end.

"Oh well," she said with a shrug, her mouth retaining its strained approximation of a smile as she glanced first at me, then Rachel, before beginning to unload the tray. "Lucky us. We get to eat everything."

* * *

Aware of Stanley's attentive eyes upon me, I felt the faintest shadow of apprehension touch me. Quite naturally he was trying to discern whether anything in the apparently inoffensive fabric of our lives might yield some hitherto hidden insight. I understood that well enough. Yet something about the intent fashion with which he now inclined his head made me wonder if the incident might be in danger of sounding rather more significant than it warranted.

"Dan has a tendency to be a little unpredictable in his moods," I said. "It was hardly a one-off. Sometimes you only have to say good morning too cheerfully to rub him up the wrong way. Annie puts it all down to hormones."

Stanley nodded several times, appearing to ponder something, before returning to his notes, and I sat in silence while he covered at least two more sides in a careful cramped shorthand. At last he dotted the final full stop with the same gesture one might use to stamp a document, before snapping the cover shut with an elastic band and securing his thoughts discreetly in his breast pocket.

It was some while after Stanley departed that the well-wishers drifted home too. Food had been kindly pressed upon us, then cleared away untouched. Annie's sister, Emma, was the last to go. She had put Rachel to bed and tidied up the kitchen before sliding a little foil blister of sleeping tablets into my hand. She would have to hurry home to relieve the babysitter, she said, but we were to call her the moment we had any news.

I saw her out before rejoining Annie, who was sitting in a trance of exhaustion at the kitchen table. It was the first time that we had been alone together all day.

"It's late," I said eventually. "We should get some rest."

Annie nodded, yet neither of us moved. It was a while before she roused herself. "He asked me if I thought it was possible Dan had run away." Her voice was stiff with indignation. "I told him there and then that Dan wasn't the kind of boy who would ever do anything like that. I said that if *that* was the line of investigation they were intending to pursue, they would be wasting their time."

"And what did he say to that?"

"That they had to explore every possibility. That they were keeping an open mind." She returned to her thoughts, her hands twisting in her lap, and despite the fact that I had begun to say something, she continued to talk over me as if engaged in a conversation primarily with herself. "Only someone who's never met Dan, who knows nothing about how close we are as a family, would suggest he might have gone of his own free will. Why on earth would Dan have run away? It's ridiculous. It doesn't make any sense." Her voice rose in a querulous tone. "I mean, I know it's the job of the police to ask questions. Of course it is. But I got the impression he just took it for granted that something, somewhere, must be amiss. Every family has its issues—I won't deny that. But there's nothing particularly out of the ordinary about us, is there? We're just a perfectly average happy family, aren't we?"

Dan's things lay all about us—an ink-stained exercise book beside my elbow, the skateboard I was forever putting outside in the garden, a pair of muddy football boots by the door.

"*Aren't we*?" she repeated, with an inflexion of rising tears.

"You can only trust your instincts," I answered, not knowing what else to offer. "After all, no one knows Dan better than you."

She nodded emphatically, several times.

"That's right," she said. "A mother knows her son." Once again she was silently weeping and a renewed wave of weariness swept over me. I thought of the bed that awaited us upstairs, wondering how we might ever muster the strength to reach it.

"But the thing is, Julian, if Dan hasn't run away . . ." Her voice quavered and broke. "I just can't bear to think that someone could have . . . might have . . ." Here she faltered, both of us leaning back, as if from the horror of the unfinished thought. I rose abruptly to close the curtains, and when I sat down again was relieved to find she was pouring herself another glass of wine, her vacant expression reassuring me that she had managed to force the thought into abeyance.

"I only wish," she went on, restlessly moving off in yet a new direction, "that I had thought to collect him yesterday afternoon. I finished early, you see. That's the thing I can't forgive myself for. I keep going over and over it in my mind. If only I had brought those test papers home, instead of staying to mark them in the staff room, I would have been able to . . ." Once again she was staring into space.

I saw that each way she turned, a new reproach reared up, each in turn prompting a hasty retreat. She had no sooner turned her mind from the tormenting possibility that she might have prevented this, than a terror that Dan was even now being held against his will had taken hold of her. And as she tried to close her mind again, up sprang the darkest fear of all, the one that could not under any circumstances be voiced: that he might no longer even be alive. We were both complicit, the two of us on the run together.

"I keep praying and praying," she said in a hoarse whisper, "that the doorbell will ring and there he'll be—just standing there." Her eyes glittered and blinked.

"Bedtime now." I drew her to her feet. "You must be shattered."

She followed obediently as I led her up the stairs. Then I undressed her while she sat shivering on the edge of the bed.

"I'll never sleep," she wept.

I pressed one of the tablets her sister had given me into her hand, and closed her fingers over it before passing her a glass of water.

"But if he comes back in the middle of the night, I might not—"

"If he comes back, I'll be here. Don't worry."

She took the tablet submissively, gulping it down with a swig of water. I slid her nightdress over her head, then she curled sideways on the bed, burrowing into the cleft of the pillow, and the comfort of the rustling cover as I drew it over her shoulders soothed us both.

"You promise that you'll wake me if . . ."

"I promise," I said, switching off the light. In the darkness I was startled to feel her reach out and draw me to her. The touch of her hands in my hair, the glancing damp of fresh tears on her cheek, and then the sudden saltiness of her tear-swamped mouth. Once the sleeping pill had taken effect, I lay wide awake as Annie slept beside me, waiting for the sound of Dan at the front door. Yet nothing in the quiet night stirred.

25

The next day, Angela Kofi arrived. A mahogany-skinned, robustly built woman, she was as vivid and gregarious as Stanley was concealed, her sheer bulk commanding the kitchen.

"Hi there, folks! I've heard all about your troubles and I'm so sorry. I feel for you. It's a terrible, terrible thing." She shook us both warmly by the hand, explaining that she was our designated family liaison officer and that she was here to offer us support and information throughout the investigation. Then she settled herself in the kitchen with all the familiarity of someone who had arrived for the duration, putting on the kettle and rifling through the cupboards until she found the biscuit tin, before coaxing Annie into a chair.

"Because your son's only twelve, he's automatically classed as vulnerable and therefore high risk. So these first few days are going to be crucial. You see, if he *has* run away—and we don't find him quickly—I'm afraid the chances of finding him at all are going to diminish very rapidly. All the statistics tell us that the likelihood of a runaway becoming caught up in drugs and criminality—of homelessness becoming a way of life—only increases with each day on the street."

Annie was shaking her head. "He hasn't run away. How many times do I have to say it? *Why will no one listen to me!*" Then she covered her face with her hands, beginning to weep as a child might, with no attempt at restraint.

"Now, now," Angela soothed, encircling Annie's shoulders while deftly withdrawing a packet of tissues from her bag with her free hand. "Don't upset yourself like this. No one's taking anything for granted, I promise you." She pulled a chair alongside Annie and handed her a fistful of the tissues. "Shall I tell you what will happen next?"

Poor Annie. She had been crying on and off all day, and her face was so swollen she was barely recognizable. She nodded several times, hiccuping down tears and attempting to dry her eyes.

"The next thing we'll do is issue a press release, okay? Try to raise public awareness. Maybe someone saw something, heard something—but hasn't yet put two and two together."

Little shuddering breaths ran through Annie as she took this in, dabbing still at her eyes.

"It's always hard to predict how responsive the press will be. The race, sex, and age of the child have a lot to do with it. I mean, horrible as this may sound, it's really only missing girls who get the media excited. Particularly white middle-class girls. The fact that Dan's a boy, that he's nearly thirteen—that's a tricky one. I have to be honest with you." She glanced at us both in turn. "However, on the plus side, he's white. He's never been in trouble with the police. And you're both professional people. Our feeling is that these factors will go in your favor. But the press can be a double-edged sword. They have to be managed properly. You're going to have to prepare yourselves for their prying." She patted Annie's hand in hers. "You might even want to think about going away for a few days. Just until it dies down."

I can still recall how we sat trying to take it all in, too dazed and confounded to say much, before Annie stumbled up from her chair as Angela's words finally registered.

"I haven't the slightest intention of going anywhere," she said, replacing the lid of the biscuit tin with an angry clatter. "If Dan came back and found no one here, I would never forgive myself."

When we woke the next morning to discover a small gathering of journalists and photographers camped outside the house the sensation of unreality only intensified. In a trance we received the well-wishers who overspilled the tiny house, and the procession of police who came and went, while the press huddled all the while at our garden gate.

Then the police took Dan's toothbrush away for DNA samples before filing a copy of his dental records, and the distressing implications were impossible to ignore. Annie agreed to make a personal appeal at the news conference they had organized. I took her by the hand and led her into a small room filled with what Angela said afterwards had been a good press turnout. Annie moved like an automaton, sitting when I touched her shoulder, staring sightlessly at the assembled journalists and cameras with no apparent awareness of where she was or why they might be there. It was with great relief that I heard her find her voice when the moment came.

"Please, Dan," she said, leaning towards the microphone, speaking in a voice that was barely a whisper, "if you're out there, call us. And if anyone watching knows anything—anything at all—please, *please,* I beg you to come forward." Then she bowed her head and wept, caught in vivid relief by the blizzard of flashlights.

That was the only occasion we left the house that week. On our return we drew the curtains against the reporters and tried not to listen as they filed their reports only a few feet from the windows. To protect us from the press, a relay of volunteers—mainly mothers of children in Rachel's class—came to take Rachel to and from school each day, while Annie and I remained in the darkened house. It was one of these volunteers who told us, in the sotto voce tones of one conversing with the recently bereaved, that she had just passed an incident vehicle set up outside Dan's school, and that there were now Missing posters pinned all about the district. Then the afternoon volunteer, returning Rachel a little later than expected, reported apologetically that she had been delayed by a police roadblock stopping anyone who passed the school to ask where they had been on the day Dan disappeared.

"When is Dan coming home?" Rachel asked unexpectedly, later that evening. Annie rose to her feet in confusion, at once busying herself about the kitchen.

"I wish I could tell you, but I'm afraid the truth is that we just don't know," I said. "We very much hope it won't be much longer."

Flicking between television channels after Rachel had gone to bed, I was just in time to catch the end of the regional news bulletin. Beyond the journalist's left shoulder, I caught a quick glimpse of our house before my fingers found the button and snapped the television off again. If the failure of our story to make the local news on the first day had perturbed me, this public acknowledgment of our plight shook me to the core.

I had always deplored the media's tendency to indulge in sensationalist accounts of crime stories. Yet here we were, having apparently slipped through a crack in our own uneventful lives to find ourselves at the center of a major police investigation.

For two days, forensic investigators dressed in hooded overalls and masks sifted painstakingly through the house for clues. At midday they stopped for lunch, removing their gloves and masks to sit gossiping over sandwiches, rather like film extras coming off duty. No sooner had they packed up and left than a computer specialist arrived, dressed formally in suit and tie, politely explaining that he had come to trawl through all the Web sites Dan had logged on to in recent months.

I had never had dealings of any kind with the police before—not even for the most minor of traffic offences—and though I knew it was absurd, I was dogged by a feeling that we didn't belong here. That we simply weren't the kind of people to whom such a misfortune happened.

Annie and I had met just as she was emerging from a prolonged period of mourning for her husband. Though still only in his mid-thirties, David Wray had died after a lengthy battle with leukemia, leaving Annie to raise their two children alone, while simultaneously struggling to hold down a job as a French teacher at a nearby sixth-form college.

It was sheer providence that brought us together. My work meant I was abroad for much of the year, but a rare assignment had taken me to London the day I came across her standing alone in the Courtauld Institute. She caught my eye immediately, for she was by anyone's standards an extremely striking-looking woman. With her dark hair and soulful brown eyes, you might have found a face like hers among the portraits of El Greco. (Later she was to tell me with a mixture of pride and amusement of the family legend that held that her mother's side were descended from Spanish pirates.) She was standing immersed in Manet's *Déjeuner sur l'herbe*, and it was the intensity of her absorption as much as her good looks that made me pause beside her.

"You must go and see the larger version in the Musée d'Orsay one day," I said with a smile.

"Oh, of course!" She turned eagerly. "I was trying to work out why it looked so familiar. I lived in Paris as a student and I suppose I must have seen it then."

At the time I simply assumed her to be an habituée of art galleries. Only later did I discover that this visit was in reality a one-off—a half-term trip intended to broaden Dan's cultural horizons. Annie for her part presumed from my "bookish manner" that I must have some kind of curatorial role at the institute, and treated me with an uncharacteristic deference. It was later a source of mutual amusement that our first meeting should have been founded on a reciprocal misunderstanding.

When I walked her to the door we found Dan sitting waiting for her on the steps outside. A slight, pallid boy with a shock of blond hair, he was quite unlike his mother in every way. In due course I was to learn that he bore a quite uncanny resemblance to his dead father. Annie explained that Dan had only got as far as the first room before declaring he had seen enough. Though I was disconcerted to discover she had a child, I offered her my card, and a few days later, to my great delight, she called.

* * *

On our first date, in an unashamed attempt to impress, I took her to a gallery where I had been involved in assessing a little pen-and-ink drawing they had recently purchased. It was believed to be the only surviving drawing by the Italian sculptor Desiderio da Settignano, and I rang them in advance to arrange the viewing. I explained to Annie that a certain stiffness in the figures had initially troubled me and, donning a pair of gloves, demonstrated how the picture's shortcomings were heightened when one turned it upside down. Right side up, the brain automatically corrects any subtle gaps in logic, but upside down, the work becomes abstract and the mistakes easier to spot. I had eventually concluded that it was a forgery.

Though in time Annie became rather more irreverent about my line of work—she once tried to provoke me by saying I was "trading in the trophies of a wealthy elite"—on this expedition she remained gratifyingly receptive. Afterwards we had a very pleasant dinner together. But though I was instantly smitten by her charms, I recognized a bruised heart when I saw one and bided my time. We went to plays and concerts together, we discussed books and poetry; in short, we forged a common bond in culture. So it was that we managed to circumvent the differences in political sensibility that were later to intrude, and little by little she succumbed to my wooing—at first cautiously but later with a reciprocal passion that quite disarmed me.

For once she took me into her bed I discovered that Annie had an unsuspected reckless quality. I was five years her junior, and she made much of being the older woman—and what she teasingly claimed to be my relative inexperience. This intoxicating charge between us soon formed a dependence in me. A dependence strong enough to keep me in her thrall long after events had all but undone us in every other way. To this day, the memory of Annie unclothed—her sheer feline grace between the sheets—can arouse an ardor, a *longing*, that no other woman has elicited in me before or since.

In all probability, this role play revealed a side she had not even suspected in herself—one that rejuvenated her after the dormant years of her husband's illness and her subsequent bereavement. The dynamics of this game soon permeated every aspect of our relationship. I played the buttoned-up conservative and she the insurgent. People often commented in a puzzled way on what an unlikely couple we made—yet our differences only charmed us, at least in those early days. She had a certain style, a whiff of something bohemian, that spoke to the treasure hunter in me, perhaps. I set about my ill-fated campaign to bring order to Annie's life, while she in turn dedicated herself to introducing some spontaneity into mine.

There came a time, some months into our relationship, when she announced that she had finally found the courage to pack up her husband's possessions—something she had never been able to contemplate before. After clearing his clothes from the wardrobe and all his books from the shelves, her newfound resolve only faltered when it came to parting with the titanium-framed bicycle that had always been his particular pride and joy. Eventually, she just left it in the shed, where Dan was later to retrieve it with such enthusiasm and claim it for himself.

Shortly after her clear out, I let out my bachelor flat in New York and moved in with Annie, both of us filled with elation at the prospect of this new chapter unfolding in what was almost by now our middle years.

I should have known what I was letting myself in for. You had only to look around the house to understand the haphazard workings of Annie's mind. Every stair was heaped with little piles intended for redistribution, though nothing was ever moved, but merely added to. The dresser in the kitchen was festooned with family photographs, together with numerous precious objects the children had made over the years. I had long since given up trying to locate anything in any of the drawers, so tangled were their contents: an extraordinary array of items retained on the unlikely off chance that they might one day prove useful. I seem to recall an entire picnic set clattering piece by piece about my ears when I was rash enough to throw open one of the overhead cabinets.

I had no sooner moved in than I learned that the chaos was further compounded by Annie's tendency to zealously commit herself to new hobbies before promptly losing interest again. Reminders of these short-lived enthusiasms were scattered everywhere about the house. Early on there was a charmingly eccentric bout of knitting, before the balls of wool and dog-eared patterns were left to gather dust in a bag that had swung ever since from the handle of the kitchen door. Shortly after, in an impulsive desire for self-sufficiency, she had taken a lease on one of the plots on the nearby allotments, producing a bumper crop of runner beans before she allowed it to run to seed, whereupon the council soon requisitioned it. The seedling trays and compost remained stacked in a moldering heap in the garden for years afterwards. Then she turned her attention to environmental matters, investing in various boxes that now blocked the kitchen and overflowed with things that, though intended for recycling, were only ever intermittently emptied.

Despite my determination to get Annie to reform her ways, she remained puzzlingly resistant, insisting with a certain feistiness that she "liked things just as they were." Perhaps I would have approached cohabitation with a little more circumspection if it had ever occurred to me that she simply didn't regard herself as someone in need of rehabilitation.

24

It was Angela who told us that the police had found something they believed to be of potential significance. Dan kept a small metal safe in his room—a birthday present from Annie—and unable to crack the code they had resorted, with her permission, to forcing the lock. Inside they found a letter addressed to Annie from his school, a list of cheats for various PlayStation games, and a torn slip of paper bearing the message *y dont u + me go out 4 sum fun? lol.*

The note had been quickly traced to a girl in Dan's class named Shania, who shamefacedly admitted she had written it in a reckless moment that she subsequently regretted, for they had had only two "dates," after which, by mutual consent, they had never spoken again. But it was the letter from school that opened the new line of inquiry. His form teacher had sent it in the post four days before his disappearance, requesting Annie to come in to discuss a general concern over slipping grades and what his teacher described as "a continuing lack of care or effort." Angela explained that the police were struck as much by what the letter contained as by the fact that he had evidently wished to conceal it from us.

It was enough to bring Chief Inspector Stanley back again. There he stood, shaking out his rain-soaked umbrella on the hearth, when with sinking hearts we opened the door to him once more.

In the kitchen he hovered with a tentative air until I pulled forward a chair for him, whereupon he sat primly, waiting while Annie made her usual prevarications, but no sooner had she taken her seat than he went to work with all the enthusiasm of a terrier routing a rabbit.

"Were you aware that Dan's attitude was causing concern at school?" he asked.

"Yes," Annie said. "Of course. Dan's schoolwork has been an issue for some time. He started secondary school only last autumn, you see, and it was taking a while for him to find his feet."

"Why didn't you mention these concerns in the first interview?"

Annie sat regarding Stanley with a faintly defiant expression.

"I didn't think it relevant," she said.

"Surely anything in a situation like this might be relevant?"

"Dan's not on trial, is he?"

"That's right. Dan's not on trial."

"I can see how quickly two and two can suddenly add up to five, that's all." She glanced sharply at me. "Look. He went from the security of a small primary school straight into the cut and thrust of a large comprehensive. It requires a big adjustment. That's all."

The decision about which school to send Dan to had been the subject of some strained debate between us, and I had always been puzzled by her final choice, for Fishers Comprehensive was a school beset by problems. A larger-than average intake of students with special needs, not to mention students for whom English was a second language, meant it had encountered severe problems recruiting new teachers. A disastrous Ofsted report had caused sufficient concern for the school to be put on special measures and a new headmaster brought in, with instructions to turn the place around.

"I'm sorry, but I honestly don't think there's any insight to be gained from going down this particular avenue," Annie said, sitting back in her chair and folding her arms as if to draw an end to the matter. Yet one glance at Stanley's face made it plain he begged to differ.

"Perhaps we might talk a little," he said courteously, "about the vending-machine incident."

Her eyes blazed in indignation

"The school had no right to give you confidential information like that! No right at all. The 'vending-machine incident,' as you call it, happened a while ago—in Dan's first term. I wasn't very amused at the time, but there it is. It's all done and dusted. He made a mistake, and we agreed to put it behind us. What good can come from resurrecting it now?"

The three of us sat in silence for a moment, becoming aware of the rain that still pattered at the window. Annie looked down at her hands, frowning when Stanley persisted.

"It's important to hear your version. It will help me to build up a picture. To fill in the gaps."

I couldn't help but watch this tussle between them with some fascination. Annie's high-minded views on education meant I had learned to broach the subject with extreme caution, yet here was Stanley, stepping in with the bold fearlessness of the newcomer, and I was astonished to see her responding with such reticence. Indeed, I had the distinct impression that she was inching around a hidden trap of some kind, yet I couldn't for the life of me work out what it might be.

At length she looked up again. "You said he wasn't on trial."

"Yes, that's right. That's precisely what I said."

They held each other's gaze for some moments more before Annie grudgingly began to speak.

"A few weeks into his first term, the deputy head called me at work to tell me that Dan had been caught stealing. It transpired that an older boy had shown him how to close the end of a loo roll before pushing it up inside the mouth of one of the school's vending machines. So when children went to buy something, they would get the item of food they wanted, but no change, and just assume the machine was broken. Then, at the end of the day, Dan and this boy were going back, removing the blockage, and filling their pockets with all the coins that cascaded down. When Dan admitted to the whole thing, I was mortified. I immediately grounded him for a week and ordered him to pay six months' pocket money to a charity of the school's choice. I have to say, though I'm not in any way trying to minimize Dan's role, that I always felt the older boy was principally to blame and had led him astray. So I was very relieved when I heard he had been suspended for some new misdemeanor shortly afterwards."

She pressed her hands together. "But you have to trust me when I say that at heart Dan's a good kid. Honestly. If he were here now, you would see for yourself. He just needs a firm hand at times. Like a lot of boys his age. It's just a phase. That's all. Just a phase."

She looked down at the table, where her fingers now restively traced the grain of wood, before meeting his eye again. "He was a great source of comfort to me in the years after my husband died."

Stanley nodded, the shadow of a sympathetic smile fleeting across his sallow features. This hint of fellow feeling seemed to shift something in Annie, for after a moment's hesitation she added in a soft voice, "I can't deny the whole thing was a wake-up call. For the first time I began to wonder if it was really the right school for him, after all."

Encouraged to see her at last letting her guard down, I thought I would prompt her still further.

"Do you remember how horrified we were by his stories when he first started there? He used to come home saying he'd seen children openly smoking joints on their way to school. That it was not uncommon for kids to be drunk or stoned in class. And pretty soon it became apparent from what he told you that bullying and petty intimidation were virtually everyday occurrences."

There was a pause while she regarded me with a cool expression.

"Julian went to Harrow and then Oxford," she told Stanley. "I think the real world has proved something of an enduring surprise ever since."

Stanley's eyes darted momentarily between us but he made no response.

"It's perfectly true," Annie went on, "that initially I was a bit concerned. Of course I was. But after the first few weeks these accounts grew less and less common—until they eventually stopped altogether. I was terribly relieved. I put it down to the fact that the new headmaster's regime must be starting to take effect. You know, I had gone to a talk he gave and been impressed. I had put my faith in him."

Stanley was busily making notes in his book, and in the silence came the sound of rain against the windows. Through a gap in the curtains my eye was caught by a group of girls in the Fishers Comprehensive uniform, huddled beneath umbrellas. They had stopped to talk to the journalists outside and were gesticulating animatedly towards the house. One of the girls began to cry, and as the others led her away with their arms about her shoulders, there was something undeniably self-conscious in the tableau they presented, as if they were only playing experimentally at grief. When one of the photographers stepped forward with a camera, they at once arranged themselves in an obliging line, posing with sad pious faces.

Annie was staring into space, lost in memories. At length she sighed heavily. "Unfortunately, it wasn't long before new issues came up and all my initial worries returned."

"What kind of issues?"

"Oh God . . ." She exhaled again. "Everything. Everything about him appeared to be changing. His language, his accent . . . his whole *attitude*," she said wretchedly. Once again she appeared to debate whether to proceed. She glanced first at Stanley and then me, the color rising in her cheeks. "I began to look around—to think about what alternatives there might be. I had heard good things about a school in the next borough. When I went to have a look, I really liked it. It was smaller, more arts-based. It had a higher intake of middle-class children. But when I told Dan about it, he was adamant he wouldn't change schools. He got terribly upset. *'The other kids will think I'm a total loser,'* he said. He told me he'd once seen a boy who had changed schools being set upon in the street by his old classmates, shouting that he was a traitor. So in the end I agreed that we would review it all when the school year ended. That if things hadn't significantly improved by then, I would have no choice but to transfer him."

Though I was careful not to betray the fact, I sat listening to all of this in some astonishment, for she had never made any mention of the possibility of a new school to me.

My tentative suggestion that she send Dan to boarding school had prompted such a high-minded lecture on state education from Annie that it was immediately apparent the subject was one best avoided. Indeed it was, as I recall, one of the first manifestations of a fault line. Annie's views on the subject of education were drawn both from her political beliefs and from her own education in an inner-city comprehensive, an experience she believed had broadened her outlook and made her a social chameleon, someone at ease with people from all walks of life and cultures. She wanted, she said, to bestow the same benefits on her own children.

While the other middle-class mothers agonized over state versus private education, Annie remained loftily aloof. We had a perfectly good comprehensive on our doorstep, she would assert crisply, as if that ended all debate on the matter. And if she experienced any feelings of unease when she first went to look around Fishers Comprehensive, she kept them to herself, several times reiterating her confidence in the reforming powers of the new headmaster.

Perhaps I suspected that her high-minded tone was a rather roundabout way of reproaching me for not being more like her husband, David, who had so readily shared her political outlook—for my own views were rather harder to pigeonhole. Indeed, by and large I considered myself to be in this—as in most things—no more than an impartial observer. My own parents had been conservative in both temperament and politics, and as the late and unexpected single flowering of their union (both of my parents had passed away while I was still in my early twenties, my mother outliving my father by only eighteen months), I had always been careful to establish a philosophical distance. They had wanted me to escape my provincial roots, and in fulfilling their social aspirations for me, the truth is I was left rather between two worlds, never quite one thing or the other. So the conclusions Annie drew from my boarding-school background seemed to me entirely stereotypical and of her own invention. She liked to claim I had lived my life among a privileged minority and that the real world, the grinding world of limited opportunities and economic hardship, was one of which I had little conception.

In time, everything became tainted by what she grew to think of as our fundamental differences in ideology. My work in the art world versus hers in the public sector. My desire to move to a more affluent neighborhood versus her insistence on remaining somewhere rooted in social diversity. In this way, the roles of traditionalist and insurgent that we had in the early days so affectionately assigned each other began to take on a rather more complex and darker hue. Her spirited idealism endeared her to me and wearied me in equal measure. I suppose she was imbued with a nostalgia for the time when there was a genuine polarity between left and right, a last link to her student days when such debates were deeply felt and meaningful. It was for this reason that throughout Dan's troubles at his new school, I resolved to stand well back and leave them to it.

So I could only look on with mute dismay at the metamorphosis that overtook Dan in those early months. First there was the rap music, whose defiant aggression began to emanate at all hours from his room. Then there had been that haircut so short he was rendered instantaneously thuggish, and the startling scent of cheap aftershave when he came down for breakfast. He began to spend time each morning—time he could ill afford—securing his tie with an absurdly swollen knot before gelling what little remained of his cropped hair into a spiky plumage. A new swagger entered his step, the same cocky bounce and roll the boys from the Fishers Estate habitually displayed, and it wasn't long before he'd also donned the infamous hoodie they favored—by now a motif for the more lawless of his generation—while his manner of speaking became gradually overtaken by a curious patois with distinctly West Indian inflections.

At first this transformation appeared to be leavened by a touch of playacting, of bluster, which amused Annie. I frequently heard her describing it to friends as a rather colorful phase. She would repeat choice expressions she had overheard him using, appearing to draw a curious comfort from the laughter they prompted. Perhaps the humor was a preemptive strike, a means of both acknowledging the pitfalls of her choice of schooling while simultaneously affirming that she wasn't about to shirk them.

After much nagging from Dan, Annie had even agreed to buy him a gold chain for Christmas from Argos. At the branch on King Street she found two pages devoted to them in the catalogue, with small knots of boys of about Dan's age standing poring over the pictures, discussing their relative merits with animation. Had it really come to this, she wondered, caught midway between amusement and despair as she queued—buying cheap jewelry for her twelve-year-old son to strut his stuff in at school?

"You're turning into a Gary!" she teased him when he unwrapped the chain on Christmas morning. She hoped the phrase might shock him and bring him to his senses, but to her dismay he had only nodded. Better a Gary than a Grunger, he agreed emphatically. He would rather die than be a Grunger.

"You haven't the foggiest clue what we're talking about, have you?" she asked, observing my blank expression as I listened to the exchange.

"None whatsoever," I affirmed, amiably slipping into my assigned role of old fogy. "You know perfectly well how much I rely on you to guide me through the foibles of modern youth."

And she at once set forth on a lively anthropological account of Garys, Grungers, Chavs, Street Rats, Emos, Trackies, and Skaters.

"Think of them as ethnic tribes, Julian," she had concluded with mock academic gravitas—at which Dan, suspecting that he was being obscurely lampooned, had stormed from the room.

It didn't take long for Annie's amused tolerance to wane. Though she despised herself for noticing, saying she knew it was tragically old-fashioned, before she could stop herself she would rush to restore a dropped "t" or correct a swallowed consonant. It became apparent that he was simply emulating the culture of conspicuous non-achievement that gripped so many of his classmates—in particular the boys. His increasingly apathetic attitude in class and his willful disregard for homework assignments allowed him to pass unchallenged among them.

I imagine it must have been then that it began to dawn on Annie that her son had embarked on a process of assimilation so fundamental it would involve erasing the very values she had most hoped to foster in him: a love of language and culture, together with the deep-rooted sense of citizenship that had been so central to her own rambunctious, chaotic, yet deeply liberal upbringing. Was it for this she had read A. A. Milne to him as a small boy, organized those occasional trips to art galleries as he grew older, and more recently still, attempted, whenever the opportunity presented itself, to engage him in social issues of the day?

I must confess that the day I accompanied Annie to discuss the vending-machine incident had been quite an eye-opener. Fishers Comprehensive turned out to be a huge dilapidated institution requiring security passes simply to get in and out of the building. On our way to the deputy head's office, I was startled to note that many of the teachers we glimpsed through classroom windows appeared barely older than their pupils. One teacher, midway through a science lesson, stood wearing a miniskirt and a pair of red stilettoes rather more suited to a nightclub, while the tired, prematurely aged face of the deputy head who spoke to us about the theft bore all the hallmarks of a long and stoical professional endurance.

Above all it was the astonishing ethnic diversity of the children that made the greatest impression. At the sound of the bell, faces of every creed and color crowded into the corridors: dark-skinned boys with cunningly shaved sections of scalp or exuberant Afros, dusky girls with elaborate cornrows, Sikh boys in neat turbans, and clusters of Muslim girls with their hair demurely covered. White children were visibly the minority. A number of the black boys wore combs stuck at jaunty angles in their wiry hair, while others sported diamond studs the size of drawing pins in their ears.

What appeared to unite them all was the West Indian patois Dan so faithfully emulated, only the expletives that littered their exchanges actually identifiable as English. And though I knew perfectly well it was absurd, I couldn't suppress a flutter of trepidation as I watched the more mature boys don mirrored shades, or baseball caps worn at an insolent angle, before stepping with a gangsterlike swagger onto the playing fields. I took care to wear a tolerant smile as they crowded jostling about us, while keeping one hand on my wallet and the other upon my BlackBerry.

Most of them were perfectly nice kids, Annie had said to me afterwards in a needlessly defensive way. A number came from extraordinarily difficult circumstances and were to be admired for their resilience. But though I knew better than to say so, the experience had been a revelation—the first time I had any real inkling of the subculture into which Dan was so rapidly being assimilated.

All of this of course was the unarticulated backdrop to our interview with Stanley, though I imagine he was a man well accustomed to reading between the lines. Outside our house, I saw that a family of five had pulled up in a battered car. They pushed their way to the front of the press and stood gazing over the hedge like doleful day-trippers, the mother and father chewing gum, their jaws working in unison. Then the father lifted up the smaller of the children for a better view, while the mother raised her mobile and took a picture of the house. Fortunately, Annie was sitting with her back to the window and remained entirely oblivious. She bit her lip, looking first at Stanley, then at me, before leaning forward with a reckless air, as if she had resolved to make a clean breast of the whole thing.

"About a month ago now, something happened that made me realize I couldn't afford to wait until the summer to decide whether or not Dan should change schools. I came back from college to find that he had tattooed his initial in blue ink on his hand. Here," she was indicating the gap between the thumb and forefinger of her left hand. "He was completely unashamed of it, cocky even, saying that he had done it himself with a compass and ink at breaktime. I was furious. Absolutely furious. We had a huge row."

She jutted her chin, as if defying Stanley to finally betray some kind of judgment, but he only nodded ruminatively.

"Like I said, he isn't a bad boy. In his heart of hearts he's still just a child. I don't know what it is that has got into him." Her eyes raked us both in turn. "But it was the tattoo that finally decided me. Every time I looked at it I thought of drug dealing and prison. I decided I must act quickly, so I rang the other school. They told me they had a waiting list—but I put Dan's name down anyway. I thought I wouldn't tell him until a place came up. That it was best to make it a fait accompli. And now . . . now all of this has happened." She gestured despairingly at Stanley and at the window, towards the journalists outside, blinking new tears away. "I only wish I'd done something about it all much sooner. It would have been one less thing to reproach myself with now."

"So is it possible that Dan intercepted that letter because he feared it would make his transfer to another school all the more likely?"

"Yes," she said in a whisper. "Yes. That thought has certainly crossed my mind."

Her distress obviously struck Stanley as no more than an habitual aspect of his daily duties, for he continued in his matter-of-fact way: "The picture you paint is of a boy displaying the kind of behavior that might well be relevant to our investigation. It suggests to me that he may well have had other issues of which you were unaware."

Annie nodded, dabbing hopelessly at the flow of tears. The balls of tissue she held in each hand were so damp by now they were crumbling into little fragments.

"Saying it all out loud to someone, hearing myself say it . . . I can't deny that it was all a bit of a mess, really."

"There is, of course, another factor to weigh up. For I think I would be right in saying that this decline in Dan's behavior also coincided almost exactly with Mr. Poulter moving in?"

"Well, yes," Annie conceded, before faltering as she registered the implication. "Though it doesn't necessarily follow that they're connected," she added in an uncertain tone.

"No," Stanley said, with an inflexion that managed to run directly counter to the words, "it doesn't *necessarily* follow that there's any connection at all."

Then they both turned in unison to fix their eyes upon me.

"Perhaps, Mr. Poulter, we might take this opportunity to explore your relationship with Dan in a little more detail."

Of course I knew perfectly well that it is standard procedure for boyfriends and stepfathers to be among the first suspects in cases like this, but I was nonetheless dismayed to find the spotlight now settling on me. I suppose I had harbored a secret hope that I had successfully seen off such a possibility in my first encounter with Stanley.

"I'm more than happy to answer whatever questions you might have," I said. "From the very outset I was eager to forge a friendship with Dan—though I would be the first to confess that my early efforts to woo him were a little ham-fisted. I remember, for example, giving him a copy of the *Iliad*, hoping it might fire in him the same passion for the classics it had done in me when I was about the same age. Are you familiar with the *Iliad*?"

Stanley nodded. "I seem to recall it from my schooldays," he said a little tersely.

"Well, Dan took one look at it and cast it to one side without a second glance. Annie had to explain that if I was hoping to win him over with a gift, I might be better advised to buy him a pair of the latest trainers." I laughed as I imparted this, hoping to demonstrate my essential humility. "I know only too well," I went on, "that I am unschooled in the ways of modern children. Until I met Annie, my constant traveling meant I had lived a largely solitary life. I was just about to take up a new contract in America, in fact, when my path so fortuitously crossed with Annie's."

I paused to take her hand, conscious of how intently they were both listening.

"And how did family life suit you?"

"It was like a breath of fresh air. Exactly what the doctor might have ordered. It certainly shook me out of my insular ways. You see, we met at a time when it had begun to dawn on me that I simply wasn't cut out to be single. And although I had never particularly wanted children of my own, when Annie introduced me to Dan, I saw a boy in need of a father figure. It struck me at once that here was a challenge—a chance to do something worthwhile."

"Very commendable," Stanley nodded approvingly. There was a pause. "So I imagine Dan's subsequent lack of gratitude must have somewhat rankled."

"I don't know what you—"

"Well, his continuing hostility to you must have somewhat undermined the nobility of your intentions."

Though Stanley's pleasant expression never faltered, the persistence of his implication was unnerving. Here was a man who appeared to believe he had much to gain by unseating me.

"I'm sorry, I'm really not sure what it is you're—"

"In our first interview we established by your own admission that certain tensions existed between you and Dan."

"Certain tensions, yes, but—"

"I mean, let's face it, you'd hardly be the first to discover that the role of stepparent pushed you on occasion to your very limits. It's a notoriously difficult role."

This allegation, so thinly clothed as sympathy, caused a tremble to start up in me. Yet knowing it would do me no favors to appear defensive, I did what I could to calm myself. With a great effort at self-control I thought I would try to impress on Stanley that though Dan and I might have had our difficulties, my relationship with his sister, Rachel, was—and had always been—an entirely congenial one. From the very first, I told Stanley, I had found her a sweet and compliant little creature, whose only desire was to please. It was with her that I had so happily resurrected the spurned notion of the *Iliad*, taking up my old copy, still annotated in my schoolboy hand, and reading it to her each evening at bedtime.

"Come now," Stanley said, brushing the story aside with the first sign of real impatience he had thus far betrayed. "Are you really trying to tell me there weren't times in the past year when the tensions between you and Dan didn't give rise to disagreements? When tempers didn't become inflamed? When things were voiced in anger that might have been better left unsaid?"

A new and alarming possibility came to me; if I continued to resist him, he might simply up the ante by announcing he was going to take me in for further questioning. I saw the dazzle of flashlights as I emerged from the house flanked on either side by uniformed police officers. It was not difficult to imagine the innuendo of the ensuing press reports, an apparently respectable art consultant, until now a pillar of the establishment, over whom a grave question mark now hovered. How alarmingly the old certainties melted away, how fragile my standing in the eyes of the world. *No smoke without fire.*

I felt Stanley's shrewd eyes appraising me. Clearly nothing but a credible display of candor would see the little man off now.

"Of course we have had our moments. This house is extremely small, and privacy can be hard to find."

I paused to take stock. It was impossible to read the damned man's face. He might have been a poker player, so blandly did he contemplate me. I resolved to redouble my efforts, the craven instinct to extract myself from unpleasantness triggering an unexpected clammy bloom of perspiration across my forehead.

"I won't deny that certain bones of contention have cropped up with a wearying regularity. Various items, for example, that are integral to my work have at some stage or other simply disappeared. In particular, I have learned that anything remotely resembling a gadget is apparently irresistible. And despite speaking to Dan about the matter on several occasions now, things still from time to time continue to vanish. He seems to have little awareness of the consequences of his actions on those around him. He will play music at full volume and become indignant when asked to turn it down. Then there's his language—not to mention the manner in which he sometimes speaks to his mother—which has on more than one occasion been a source of some friction between us. I won't pretend that in these moments I haven't had occasion to recall the order of my former life and wonder whether I am entirely suited to the cut and thrust of family life . . ."

Stanley's eyes were narrowing as I trailed to an uncomfortable halt. It was only then I realized that at some point Annie must have slid her hand from mine. I leaned back in my chair, crossing then uncrossing my arms.

"All a bit frazzling for you, I can see that," Stanley observed eventually, in his dry way.

Why could I not shake him off? Behind that mask, crafty machinations continued to turn. There was a bad smell in the room, as if a lid had been lifted on a drain. Added to which the lack of air was making it difficult to think straight. It was perfectly obvious what he was hoping for. Revelation. Confession. *We got into a fight, you see—I struck the boy with a poker and you'll find his body buried in the cellar.*

"Of course it stung me when he made his dislike for me so apparent," I said, my voice rising despite myself. "But if it's tales of cruelty or domestic violence you're hoping for, you'll be sorely disappointed. I never once lifted my voice, let alone a finger, to the boy . . ."

We sat in silence for some moments, the tension seeming to cast a spell of paralysis upon the room. Through the gap in the curtains I saw that a truck with a satellite dish on top was pulling up outside, causing a ripple of activity to stir through the ranks of the press. Glancing at the clock, I realized they must be preparing for the evening bulletin—and the desperation that rose in me was that of a creature at bay upon finding every escape route barred by hungry predators.

Annie stood up and went to the sink. She let the water run for a moment, before dousing her eyes. Then she buried her face in a towel, remaining so still that Stanley and I both watched her, spellbound.

"It's been a long day," he said, hastily recalling himself with a start. "You must get some rest now, Mrs. Wray." He ceremoniously closed up his notebook as he spoke, clipping his pen to his breast pocket, before running a bony finger along his tie.

"Please rest assured," he said, as he got to his feet and bowed courteously to both of us in turn, "that if there are any new developments, you will be the very first to be informed."

After Stanley left, the two of us moved in silence about the kitchen. Annie poured herself a generous glass of whiskey, appearing deep in thought. Though there was much I wished to say, I couldn't seem to frame the opening words—and the longer and more burdened the silence between us grew, the more the right opening shrank from me. The rain had died down now, and the only sound was that of water running through the guttering.

"I had no idea," I burst out so unexpectedly and with such vehemence, it took us both by surprise. "No *idea* that you were even considering other schools, let alone that you had already found an alternative and put Dan's name down for it. I was most taken aback. Did you never think to mention it to me?"

She swilled the amber fluid in her glass, prodding the ice cubes with a desultory finger.

"I can't really explain it," she muttered. "Looking back, I think I must have been in some strange state of denial about the whole thing."

"Denial?" I reiterated, coming to sit opposite her. "What on earth do you mean?"

She kept staring into her glass.

"Our lives are so hectic," she said. "I suppose I couldn't see the wood for the trees. It was only when I was trying to explain it all to the chief inspector that I realized how horribly negligent I must appear." She looked up, her eyes brimming with unshed tears. "Perhaps I couldn't bear to lose face by admitting that Dan's problems at school might be anything more than passing. Perhaps I was afraid you'd say it was no more than I should have expected—that I'd put my principles before my child."

"Do you really think that there's some connection between Dan's problems at school and his disappearance, then?"

"I don't know, Julian," she answered in a lifeless voice. "I only know that I let things drift for far longer than I should have done. Anyway," she went on, rising abruptly to her feet and beginning to clear the table, "I was pretty taken aback myself when you said you weren't sure if you were suited to family life . . . Surely that's something you could have discussed with me? Instead, the first person you confide in is a police officer."

"I would have thought it pretty obvious," I retorted, "that I was speaking under duress. If I'd insisted on an impeccably happy homelife, Stanley might have tried to put the wind up me by taking me down to the station for further questioning."

"So it wasn't true, then?"

"Of course not."

At this she nodded but did not respond, becoming lost in thought again. I watched her from the corner of my eye, hoping this meant we had reached a truce. I wanted to ask what she had made of Stanley's sly suggestion that there might be some link between my arrival in their lives and Dan's troubled behavior, for I was still smarting from the notion that I might in any way have been a source of disruption to the family. Yet, fearing that her irritation might prejudice her answer, in the end I said nothing.

"Well, one thing's for sure," Annie muttered darkly, as she returned the whiskey bottle to the cupboard. "That man certainly knows how to put the cat among the pigeons."

How humiliating it was when a colleague informed me that one of Stanley's men had contacted my office the very next morning to check my alibis. Fortunately, they were unassailable; from first thing in the morning of Dan's disappearance until an hour before my return at nine thirty, every moment of my day could be accounted for. The inquiry moved on, my reputation remained untarnished. But though I should have been thankful, I think both Annie and I knew that a shadow had fallen between us.

As that first week unfolded, the friends and neighbors who came and went provided a welcome distraction. Some came with food to sustain us, while others recounted stories of children who had disappeared, only to be miraculously returned unharmed. And every morning the post brought touching cards of support and sympathy, some from people we knew, but most from complete strangers who had read of our story in the papers. It shames me now to recall that we never responded to a single one, always thinking we would wait for the moment when we had good news to share. Rather less welcome were the scrawled, semiliterate missives with disquieting claims of psychic insight into Dan's fate, or spiteful outpourings about Annie's supposed negligence. Very soon it was easier to set them all aside unopened. So it was that as that first week drew to a close and no new developments of any kind were forthcoming, for the first time the despair began to outweigh the hope.

Neither of us could bring ourselves to attend the reconstruction in which one of Dan's classmates retraced his route home. I remember finding Annie standing in the kitchen that morning. She was weeping quietly as she ceremoniously tipped the chicken Kiev she'd bought for Dan's supper into a Tupperware box. She explained that she'd moved it fretfully around the fridge all week, unable to bring herself to throw it away, before realizing she could continue to keep it in a state of readiness by putting it in the freezer.

When Dan was transferred from the local to the national Missing Persons Bureau, there was a television appeal on *Crimewatch* that we were careful to avoid and that elicited no further information. Perhaps someone at school mentioned it to Rachel, because the next day she asked about Dan again.

"Well, it turns out," I heard Annie say in a rush of words before I had time to intervene, "that he's gone away for a bit. Just for a little while . . . On a kind of holiday."

I looked at her in astonishment, though she refused to meet my eye.

"So why are all those people outside our house then?" Rachel asked, frowning deeply.

"Yes, it's very odd, isn't it?" Annie said, buttering a piece of toast with careful deliberation. "I keep wondering the same thing. But if we're lucky they'll all get bored before too long and go away again."

Rachel's frown only deepened, as she tried to fathom this. The words told her one thing and Annie's evasive manner another. Her penetrating gaze rested on both of us in turn for some moments, though to my great relief she asked nothing more.

For a few days the journalists and photographers swelled in number. One morning we woke to find a letter on the mat from the *Mail* offering a substantial sum for exclusive rights to our story, and it was only the firm intervention of Angela Kofi that prevented me from storming out to confront the journalist who had delivered it.

When police divers arrived to search the nearby stretch of river, the ranks of press swelled still further, their buzzing anticipation that of spectators with a ringside seat who sense the main event is at last about to begin. But when the divers failed to find anything, an air of defeat crept into their increasingly sporadic news reports. There was to be no dramatic denouement, after all. The storyline was running dry on them.

For a while, the lack of progress itself became the story. Snippets of their pieces to camera floated up to us. "Family and friends remain baffled by the disappearance." "Two weeks after Dan Wray was last seen, there have been no major leads, no confirmed sightings." Then a sprinkling of headlines signaled the conclusion of their interest—*HOPE FADING FOR TEACHER'S MISSING SON*, and day by day the numbers of journalists fell away. One morning we woke to find the street once again deserted.

23

In time, the well-wishers who had seen us through the early stages also drifted away again, drawn by the commitments of their own lives. Without their comings and goings the house felt unnervingly quiet. Though Angela continued to keep us up-to-date on the inquiry, as each new avenue drew a blank, her detailed reports made for dispiriting listening.

Little by little, I stopped urging Annie to be positive and began instead to remind her how important it was to be strong for Rachel's sake. She did what she could to put a good face on things, appearing to rally on Rachel's return from school, but no sooner was her daughter in bed than Annie would retreat into herself again.

One evening I was crossing the landing when I glimpsed her through a crack in the bathroom door. She was sitting on the edge of the bath, muttering something in an imploring undertone. Her eyes were closed, and her fingers tightly interlaced as if one hand sought solace while the other offered it. It was a scene so intensely personal, I instinctively turned and crept away.

Soon Annie began to dwindle before my eyes, her lovely face growing gaunt and waxen. I took to cutting her food into small pieces, and sometimes even to coaxing a morsel or two between her lips. Angela suggested soup, and this became the only thing that sustained her.

I had always prided myself on being a rock in times of crisis and set about dusting down my modest repertoire of dishes that had served me so well as a bachelor, cooking Rachel her supper before bathing her and putting her to bed each evening. Meanwhile, Annie would sit downstairs with the noise of the television washing over her. I frequently came down at midnight to switch it off and bring her half stupefied to bed.

As the days dragged on and still no news came, Annie no longer spoke unless directly addressed. At night she stopped going to bed at all, but stayed up, playing patience on the computer, sometimes falling into an exhausted sleep only as dawn broke. Often I would come down to find her fast asleep on the sofa with her face pressed into an old sweat-shirt of Dan's. One morning when I roused her, she held the garment out to me in distress. "Every day the scent of him is getting fainter." She brought it up to her face, nuzzling among its folds. "It's as if he's slipping further and further away from me," she wept, her words muffled in the fabric.

Though Annie had grown fearful of leaving the house, I eventually managed to persuade her to see her doctor, who prescribed antidepressants, though he warned it might be a little while before they took effect. Fortunately, by the time I had to return to work she had rallied enough to resume Rachel's school run, and I could only hope this modest routine would be enough to provide her with some purpose and shape to her day.

It was around this time that she remembered an incident that had occurred when Dan was only four, and which she now saw had foreshadowed this much larger event. Her husband, David, was in hospital undergoing the first of a series of tests that were to lead to his diagnosis of leukemia, and she, by now heavily pregnant with Rachel, had taken Dan to the local park. They had stopped at the lake to feed the ducks, before she had strolled on, with Dan riding his tricycle just a little way behind. Now and then she would pause to let him catch up, until the moment came when she turned to find only an empty path. At once she hastily retraced her footsteps, expecting at any moment to encounter him. Yet at each turn there was still no sign of him. Losing her head completely, she zigzagged between the path and the woodlands that skirted it, trying to simultaneously cover each and every potential hiding place.

"Have you seen a little boy on a tricycle?" she asked breathlessly of every passerby, trying to contain her impatience at the slow, puzzled fashion in which each person in turn shook their heads. "He's only four."

And then, Dan had rounded the corner again, pedaling with gusto, while close behind him walked an elderly woman, watching over him. She had smiled when she saw Annie. "Is he yours?"

"Oh yes! Yes, he is!" Annie exclaimed, plunging to her knees like a penitent and taking him in her arms.

How wonderful that moment had been, when everything was made instantly right with the world again. Yet it was the terrible sensation that had preceded that moment, as if a limb had been abruptly severed—from which there was, this time, no relief.

One night, perhaps a month or so after Dan's disappearance, I arrived home later than usual to find Rachel fast asleep upstairs and Annie sitting in virtual darkness at the kitchen table. This was not in itself unusual. I noted with some despondency that she was drinking whiskey again, and walked about for a while, snapping on lights and drawing the curtains, trying to reinstate a little warmth and comfort into the house. She confirmed indifferently that she hadn't yet eaten, so I rifled through the spartan contents of the fridge, where I found eggs only marginally past their sell-by date and whipped up an omelette for us both. She sighed when I set the plate before her, poking halfheartedly at the food before pouring herself another generous slug of whiskey.

"Bad day?" I asked reluctantly, and she shrugged. Recently, I had become aware of a rather shameful torpor overcoming me at moments like this—and though I did what I could to stifle the fatigue, my reserves of consolation and reassurance were undeniably running low.

"Want to talk about it?"

She shook her head, and I ate while she sat staring at her plate. Even after I had cleared the table she still retained the same posture, and it was only as I was beginning to wash up that I realized she had finally spoken.

"I can't stop thinking about all the mistakes I've made," she said, when I asked her to repeat herself.

"Mistakes?"

"When the inspector asked me to describe Dan, I was surprised by how difficult I found it. It's preyed on my mind ever since. Because the truth is . . . the truth is that in many ways he had become a bit of a mystery to me. It's an odd thing for a mother to say, I know, but I can't think of any other way of putting it." She fell silent again, and I had the impression I so often had now that she was talking more to herself than to me.

"The police brought some of Dan's things back today."

Annie pulled a pair of battered notebooks from a plastic bag and set them side by side on the table before us.

"Look."

They were the pair of diaries that together spanned Dan's first year of secondary school up until his disappearance. In the initial stages of their investigation the police had scoured them carefully before concluding that they contained little of any value to their investigation.

"Oh Annie. You've been busy reading them?"

"Well." Her laughter was bleak. "He's not exactly Samuel Pepys. I mean, there's scarcely anything to them, really—most of the pages are blank. It's just the odd line here and there. But if you can overlook the atrocious grammar and spelling . . . sometimes there's an occasional entry, the odd phrase that is really quite . . . quite touching."

I sat down beside her, and we began to turn the pages together. The first diary covered the camping holiday the three of them had taken in Spain the summer before Dan started at Fishers Comprehensive. "That's where those lovely pictures were taken." She nodded towards two photographs pinned to the fridge. *Having a wiked time* was all he'd written for the entire period. "You see—he was happy then," she said, her spirits reviving a little.

The pages were blank for all of September. "New school. Who can guess what was going through his mind?" she murmured, leafing through. In all probability very little, I thought to myself. In the two years I'd known him, Dan had hardly struck me as a boy of hidden depths.

In October—*5 Days till my Birthday. 4 Days till my Birthday. 3 Days till my Birthday. 2 Days till my Birthday. MY BIRTHDAY!* "Ah!" Annie said tenderly. "And suddenly he was twelve."

Then page after empty page again. Finally in January—*After school, get geko food.* The next day—*Meet up wid obi.*

In February—*skool sucks!* Later on in February—*HALF TERM! Stil need to get geko food. Chemistry hw. New trainers.* Later on, once again—*BOARING! I hate skool.*

By the end of that same month he had received the invitation from Shania and noted it with an exuberant row of exclamation marks, together with more exclamation marks on the actual day of their meeting.

"First date and not a word to his mother," Annie said, that private smile, the one that appeared to express a depth of love only her children could tap in her, twitching at the corners of her mouth.

By March, the intimations of adolescence were growing—*Don't think anyone likes me. Mrs. Spag Bol was ill (is this world real?)*

"I obviously completely underestimated him," she said. "I mean, look at the excitement all those exclamation marks reveal about his first date. I had no idea he was beginning to be interested in girls. Not a clue! And then there's the heartbreaking insecurity in that reference to not being liked. And the question about the reality of the world. Who would have thought he was having metaphysical doubts like that! You know, it all suggests a sensitivity . . . a capacity for soul-searching that I'm ashamed to admit I was completely oblivious to."

I couldn't help but wonder at how she could weave so much out of so little. Yet I made no comment, too saddened to meet her eye.

"Of course," she went on, "I know perfectly well that children become more secretive as they grow older. I just need to look back to my own teenage years. But he's still only twelve. I suppose I hadn't expected it quite yet." She closed the books, cradling them to her. "I know it's ridiculous, but it's hard after all those years in which he was so dependent on me for everything, to find I have become so . . . so marginal. And then there are all the things that seem to be missing. No hint of any plan to run away. No suggestion of any motive. Surely if he had been planning such a thing, you would expect to find some kind of clues, however veiled?"

"There are, of course, those two rather hostile references to his school," I offered, though I at once regretted it, for her head dropped forwards, and after a long silence, a pattering of tears fell onto the cover of one of the diaries.

"Yes," she said at length, as if we had arrived at last at the heart of the matter. "Yes, that's true. Everything seems to keep coming back to that bloody school, doesn't it?"

As Dan's first term at Fishers Comprehensive progressed and he became increasingly taciturn, despite Annie's frequent urging to bring one of his classmates home for tea, he had returned every evening alone. She looked about her modest home for answers.

"Is there something about the way we live that embarrasses you?" she asked him one day.

He had glanced at the book-lined shelves, at the *Guardian* left open on the kitchen table and the reproductions of contemporary paintings on the wall with a fleeting but unmistakable disdain.

Indeed, in the entire eight months he had been at the school, Annie could only once recall his bringing someone home: an undernourished-looking boy called Jamie, who had asked plaintively after tea if he could stay the night. Of course, she'd agreed, pleased by the request, just as long as Jamie checked with his mother. But he had shaken his head. "She's away."

"Well, someone must be looking after you?"

Not really, he replied with a shrug. His mother had left some money for takeaways and told him to keep out of trouble. Further questioning revealed that they were living in a women's refuge nearby, though he was strictly forbidden to say exactly where. His mum had told him if he didn't keep his mouth shut, he'd have his dad on the doorstep again, and there was no way he was risking that. Annie asked if his father had been violent, but he wouldn't be drawn any further.

That night, Jamie had undressed for bed to reveal shockingly frayed and grubby underwear. Annie had given him a pair of clean pajamas before taking his clothes away to be washed and pressed ready for the morning. Over breakfast she attempted to insist Jamie stay with us until his mother returned, but he'd proved evasive, and the following day Dan had returned from school without him.

It was only some days later that Annie realized the state-of-the-art digital camera I had given her for her birthday was missing. To my great irritation, she refused point-blank to raise the issue with Dan. It was too delicate, she insisted. What if it hadn't been Jamie after all? It would be unforgivable to start throwing unfounded accusations about. Poor

Dan would never dare bring another friend home again. Perhaps she was right to be so cautious, for when I took Dan to one side to question him about the matter myself, he had stormed off in a huff, slamming the front door behind him with enough force to rattle the windows.

After that, Dan never mentioned Jamie again, and Annie presumed, with relief, that the friendship had foundered. She formed an impression that Dan had made a new alliance with a boy named Obi, whom she met only once, quite accidentally, when she happened to be passing just as the two of them were emerging from school one day. To Dan's patent mortification, she had pulled over to offer them both a lift. Obi stood out among the crowds of schoolchildren, she said, a strikingly handsome boy of Afro-Caribbean descent, sporting large diamond studs in each ear, with a wide disarming smile. She sounded so pleased when she reported the encounter to me later, so determined to be taken by him, I saw this was exactly the type of multicultural friendship she had had in mind when she first put Dan down for the school.

It was only through the police that she discovered their friendship had been rather less of a desirable thing than she had supposed. For during their initial search of Dan's room, the police had uncovered a bin liner filled with hubcaps that Obi had admitted were part of an ongoing competition between them to see who could steal from the most prestigious cars. They also found a drawer of half-empty aerosol cans that Obi readily explained were for their other favorite afterschool activity of spray-painting their tag name in inaccessible locations about the neighborhood.

Annie stood up slowly, and went to put the diaries away in one of the drawers in the dresser before going to pour herself a little more whiskey.

"Obi told the police they were creating street art, do you remember? One of the officers who interviewed him the other day described him to me afterwards as a 'likable rogue.' Could charm the birds out of the trees, he said." She smiled a rueful smile to herself and then sighed deeply, appearing at once drawn and defeated.

22

When I came home from work the next day, I found Annie startlingly transformed. She was standing at the cooker preparing supper, which in itself was something of a new departure. A little color had returned to her cheeks, and she was no longer wearing the sagging tracksuit that had become her customary attire. Glancing about the room, I noted too that the table was piled with newly purchased groceries. It was at once apparent, from the eager way in which she now leaned against the cooker and folded her arms, that she had something she was impatient to impart.

"You're not going to believe this, Julian, but this afternoon on my way back from the shops, I bumped into Obi. There he was, coming out of the school gates just as I was driving by."

Though it flashed through my mind that it was rather more likely that something about our conversation of the previous evening had prompted her to deliberately seek him out, I contented myself with merely raising an eyebrow. "He must have been pretty surprised to see you."

"Yes," she agreed. "He was trying to act very cool in front of his friends, but yes, I think he was pretty freaked out!"

The moment she saw Obi, Annie parked the car, catching up with him a few minutes later as he was about to cross the road to the bus stop. She told him she had some questions he might be able to help her with, and though she was aware of a sniggering among his friends, she kept her eyes fixed only on him. "I was just wondering if there was anything more you could tell me about Dan—about what you think might have happened that day after he left you."

Obi shook his head, his quick glances passing nervously over her face and away again.

"Like I told the feds, I don't know nuttin."

The other boys were jostling one another in order to better overhear their conversation, and Annie had felt dwarfed and foolish as she walked among them. Most of them had their hoods up, striding with the same rolling gait Dan had cultivated. Everything they wore appeared to be slipping from them; the crotches of their trousers hanging at knee level, their jackets falling about their arms like shawls, their caps somehow balanced on the side of the head—each item conspiring to create an impression of a pronounced and cartoonlike nonchalance.

"Can we talk privately?" Annie begged, desperation overcoming her. And at last Obi came to a halt, swinging round to face her and planting his feet with his hands thrust deep in his pockets, before nodding at the others to move on.

"Is there anything you were afraid to tell the police? No one need ever know it came from you. I give you my word."

But he only shook his head again, appearing diminished and vulnerable without his friends looking on. He licked his lips, looking away down the street for some moments as if composing himself.

"On me life. He was me blud. Me mate, yeh. I told them. I said good-bye to im. We was right here, yeh. Just where you and me is right now. He goes 'See ya tomorra,' right, and off he goes on his bike. That was it. End of story. Swear to God."

Whether from emotion, or from the cold wind that whipped past them, she thought she glimpsed the glitter of tears in his eyes, and it was as if a hand clutched her heart. It struck her that in speaking to Obi she was finally addressing the unfathomable quality of her own child.

"Was there any reason—any reason at all that you know of—why he might have run away?"

Once again he shook his head miserably.

"Maybe he had issues at home? Something he might have felt able to confide in you, but not to me?"

"No, man. The feds ask me that. I'm tellin you, he was just his normal self, right? Weren't nothin goin on far as I know. If I knew somethin, I'd tell you."

She scribbled her phone number for him on a scrap of paper, the wind tearing at it in her hand, and he had taken it before turning to resume that odd bouncing gait in the direction of his friends, who stood waiting for him a little way off. She watched the throng of boys congregate about the bus stop, a burst of horseplay breaking out as one boy seized another in an armlock and the two of them stumbled into the road, oblivious to the passing cars that tooted their horns as they swerved to avoid them. But Obi sat apart on a nearby bench, with his shoulders hunched and his head in his hands. Perhaps he too was in mourning, she thought, looking on from afar, and though their conversation had yielded so little, she found a wintry solace in his dejection as she turned towards the car.

For a short while after that, Annie appeared to recover something of her old spirit. As we moved into a second month, she announced that she was going to travel round the neighborhood and replace any missing posters that had been torn or blown away. That weekend, Rachel and I offered to join her and we drove from place to place, stopping to add an extra one whenever a new location presented itself.

"Isn't Dan still on holiday then?" Rachel asked, as the three of us worked together to attach the first of the posters to a prominently sited tree. Her eyes were hovering anxiously over the *MISSING* caption printed in bold red lettering.

Caught off guard, Annie appeared to gabble the first panic-struck words that came into her head. “No. Or rather yes, yes, he is,” she said in a brittle, cheery tone. “Only that naughty brother of yours has forgotten to tell us exactly where he’s gone, you see.”

Rachel opened her mouth as if to ask more, before appearing to decide that any further questions would contravene some unspoken taboo.

The exchange only made a dismal task more dismal still, the skies above us a lowering gray with sometimes a smattering of rain. Most people passed by without a second glance, and even those who did pause offered only the most cursory of inspections, before hurrying on their way.

MISSING—Daniel Wray
Can you help?
Daniel is 12 and disappeared on 15 April 2004
sometime around 3:15 p.m. He was last seen setting off on
his bicycle from Fishers Comprehensive in the direction of
his home in Fishers Meadows. No one has seen him since.
Daniel’s family are extremely concerned
about him and would appreciate information of any kind.
His mother and sister are desperate for news and ask
him to get in touch. They love and miss him and want
to be reassured that he is safe and well.
Daniel is 5ft 1ins tall, and of slight frame.
He has fair hair, blue eyes, and a self-made tattoo of a
D on his left hand between his thumb and forefinger.

If you have seen Daniel, please call the confidential National Missing Persons Helpline on Freephone 0500 700 700.

Flying home from foreign trips, I had once looked down on London's urban sprawl and marveled at how this teeming and disparate entity could form such an orderly and cooperative whole. Now it appeared that there were hidden cracks in the city's fabric through which a child might vanish without a single clue to mark their passing.

Still the weeks passed and no new developments of any kind emerged. It didn't take long for Annie's spirits to sink again. When the sixth-form college where she taught French extended her compassionate leave from two months to three, I couldn't help but wonder whether she was wise to accept. For while Rachel was away at school she would often sit in Dan's attic bedroom, lost in melancholy brooding. I discovered this only when I came home early one day. Having searched each room in turn, I finally found her sitting at the end of his bed. We had both jumped in alarm at the sight of each other.

"What on earth are you doing up here?" I asked.

"Oh, you know—just thinking about things," she whispered, her eyes remaining downcast on her lap.

One night I awoke with a start and lay for a moment in some confusion with my heart pounding in my chest. Slowly,

I began to make out the outline of Annie sitting upright beside me, the lamp from the street beyond creating a halo of light about her. Turning to the illuminated dial of the alarm clock I saw it was not yet three a.m.

"Annie?"

No response.

"What's going on? Are you all right?"

She was raising something to her lips, and I caught the quick petrol scent of whiskey.

"How will I bear it?" she said at last in an indistinct voice. "How can I go forward as if nothing . . ." Then an eerie keening broke from her, the very same sound that had woken me, and she began to rock to and fro, hugging her knees. "I didn't keep him safe. Didn't watch over him as I should have done. I've no one to blame but myself." Twice she struck out at the pillows. "First my husband, and now my son."

Still stupefied from sleep, I couldn't seem to marshal my thoughts, reaching out instead to try and soothe her in the darkness.

"Annie, Annie, please try to calm yourself."

It was a while before I managed to elicit from her, through her hiccuping sobs, that it was the anniversary of David's death—and she had no sooner imparted this information than her weeping escalated into wails. Then she collapsed sideways on the bed before sliding to the floor, rose up, and fell down again. It was pointless to remonstrate—I realized she had drunk far too much to be capable of rational discussion.

Over the past weeks I had been initiated into the extraordinary variation of her tears. But this was something entirely new—a shuddering, gulping storm, water flooding from her eyes, her nose, and even her mouth. It was as if she were hemorrhaging despair. She cried so much that the hair soon lay stuck all about her face in sodden snake coils. At some point she even stumbled against the wardrobe, her head striking the wood with a ghastly thud, and at my wit's end, I rang a private medical service. I couldn't think what else to do.

Thankfully, a doctor came within the hour and administered a powerful sedative, after which she slept soundly and without stirring. She was still asleep when I left for work the next day, and as I hastened to and fro getting both myself and Rachel ready for the day, I told her that Mummy was in bed with a touch of flu. Afterwards, though she sported a black eye for some days, neither Annie nor I ever referred to that night again.

Once Annie's compassionate leave elapsed, she returned to work without resistance. I think it was clear to her by now that the structure of the working day was the only thing that might stand between her and madness. At the end of the first day she returned home with a collection of little gifts and cards from her colleagues. None of her students had made any direct reference to what had happened—some stricken with awkwardness, others by a moist-eyed sympathy—and she wished she could have thought of something to say to put them at their ease. It wasn't long though before people relaxed again in her company and though she understood that this was perfectly normal—had always believed she would welcome it once they did—she was dismayed to discover how much she resented the implication that normal life must resume.

Though I watched Annie closely, I found it impossible to judge whether she was finally entering a period of grieving, or still resolutely waiting. On her return each evening she remained in a state of perpetual activity, either busying herself about the house, or tending assiduously to Rachel. Perhaps there was forgetfulness to be found in ceaseless toil. Certainly the zeal with which she now committed herself to Rachel struck me as much a bid for atonement as the natural desire to keep her safe. And who could blame her? I imagine her greatest fear was that she might lose her one remaining child.

There was a difficult period, shortly after that, when Rachel became reluctant to go to school. As the moment to depart drew nearer, she would grow tearful and cling to one of us, pleading that she be allowed to stay at home. Annie took to offering Rachel a dab of her perfume to wear on the sleeve of her school uniform, and when this no longer did the trick, allowed her to choose an inexpensive item from her jewelry box to keep in her pocket as a talisman, and in time Rachel's anxiety eased again.

Annie's hawklike vigilance over child-care arrangements was unstinting, and in many ways Rachel seemed relieved by the constraints that now surrounded her, seldom asking if she could join her friends as they played outside or to visit them in their homes. One day she showed me a silver bracelet her mother had just given her, and I noted with a pang that it was engraved along one side with Annie's phone number and e-mail address.

21

It wasn't long before it became apparent that the police investigation was running out of steam. After one of Angela's visits, in which there had, yet again, been nothing of any significance to report, we were walking across the meadows with Rachel running just ahead, when Annie turned with an abrupt indignation, to address me. "The thing is, if Dan were dead, I would know, you see. I would feel it."

I had become accustomed to these apparent non sequiturs in which she unexpectedly gave voice to one of the anxious inner debates that I suspect continually plagued her. I only nodded. Poor Annie. I hadn't the heart to challenge her. It was a relief simply to be out in the fresh air with her again, that she had, after four months, finally consented—albeit with her phone clasped at the ready—to resume our evening walks. So we strolled beside the river, taking in the glorious sunset, and nothing more was said.

The following evening, however, I had no sooner stepped through the front door than she had flown out of the kitchen to greet me.

"I've been thinking," she said.

I set down my briefcase, flexing my cramped hand.

"Do you remember all that business with the bicycle?"

"Business with the bicycle?"

"You know—you must remember."

I hung my jacket up and unhooked the tie from round my neck before glancing warily at her. There was something distinctly odd about her demeanor—the word that came to mind was "overwrought"—and I noted with foreboding how her eyes glittered as she spoke.

"I'm not quite sure I follow you, no." I walked through into the kitchen. "What business with the bicycle?" I opened the fridge and took out a bottle of wine, pouring myself a generous glass, before falling into a chair. It had been a long day. My resources were low. Perhaps we needed a holiday. Annie was leaning against the kitchen counter, frowning.

"David's old bicycle used to be kept in the shed. And one day we got home to find that Dan had gone and dragged it out again."

She watched me, waiting for the penny to drop.

"Don't you remember how obsessed he became with it? How inexplicable it seemed, particularly since the bike was still too big for him?"

Her agitation compelled her into motion, even though

the confines of the kitchen allowed only a few paces before she had to turn and retrace her steps.

"And then it suddenly occurred to me that the day he got it out of the shed was the same day you . . ."

I nodded, rubbing my eyes.

"The same day I moved in," I said, finishing the sentence for her. "Of course I remember, Annie. It was blocking the hall when I arrived. It was a struggle to get my suitcases past it. How could I forget?"

"*It was blocking the hall when you arrived!* Just think about that for a moment," she appealed in a triumphant tone. "No sooner does a rival to his father attempt to move in, than Dan—"

"Than Dan revives his father's trusty old steed in an attempt to foil me!"

"Don't mock me! I hate it when you do that," she cried, slapping the palm of her hand against the table.

"You don't think you might be making a bit too much of the whole thing?"

She leaned back against the counter again, regarding me with a thoughtful expression.

"I suppose it was just a reminder that at some level he must still have been processing his father's death. That's all."

More than anything I had come to dread her tears, and did what I could to smooth things over before retiring early to bed, leaving Annie sitting in front of the computer immersed in the Internet. When I kissed the top of her head, she blew a distracted air kiss, but her eyes never left the screen. I fell asleep lulled by the whirr of the printer and awoke briefly in the small hours of the morning to hear it still printing pages, before stretching my legs into the empty space beside me and tumbling backwards into sleep again.

In the morning I came down to find little piles of paper stacked across the kitchen table. It was Saturday, and Rachel and I ate a leisurely breakfast before strolling down to the river, leaving Annie still fast asleep. On our return we found her brewing coffee at the cooker. She said she had been awake until the early hours of the morning surfing the Internet for anything she could find about the effects of bereavement on young children.

"There's so much stuff. It's quite extraordinary. Once I started, it was almost impossible to stop." She began tidying the sheaf of printed pages. "And then as I read, all kinds of things I'd never properly considered before began to fall into place."

David's final months had been punctuated by a series of emergency admissions to hospital, each one expected by the doctors to be the last, only for him to recover enough to return home again. It wasn't until the fourth admission that he finally died. The morning afterwards, Annie sat the children down and took their hands in hers.

"Last night," she began tentatively, pausing to let Rachel yawn widely. "Last night, a very sad thing happened." Now she had their full attention, their grave eyes upon her, she was overcome with dread at the words that must come next. "Daddy," she said carefully, commanding her voice to remain steady. What phrase would best communicate this devastating event to them—would soften it, without denying its irrevocability? "Daddy went to sleep—and didn't wake up."

"You mean he's dead?" Dan asked, and she had nodded, blinking quickly to stem the tears. He stood for a moment with an odd glassy expression before turning and running from the room. But Rachel had only shrugged matter-of-factly.

"Never mind, Mummy," she'd offered by way of friendly solace, taking up her dolls again and soon becoming immersed in play. After that, Dan had refused to discuss the matter again. Though Rachel would occasionally ask when Daddy would be coming home, any attempt to raise the subject with Dan was met by resolute stonewalling.

"On the day of David's funeral—I probably never told you this before—but do you know what I did? I asked my sister to take the children to the zoo."

Annie was shadowing me about the kitchen, holding forth with exactly the same intensity as the night before.

"And quite right too," I said, guiding her to a chair and beginning to set out her breakfast. "You wanted to shield them. They were so young. Dan was only six, wasn't he? So Rachel must just have been a toddler, for Christ's sake."

But she batted my assurances away impatiently, her eyes rounded in mortification.

"The funeral was an opportunity for them to say goodbye, Julian. There are pages and pages on the importance of ritual. All kinds of suggestions about how children might help choose the clothes the dead parent is buried in, or put a keepsake in the coffin. And I—I in my great wisdom sent them to the zoo . . ."

She wrapped her arms about herself.

She remembered how Dan had been plagued by nightmares in the months that followed David's death. He would wake in terror, often saying he had dreamed that an angel had fallen from the sky to smother him. Annie couldn't imagine where he might have come by such a notion.

David had been away in hospital so much in those last few months he had scarcely been part of the children's lives anymore. In all likelihood, she decided, their father would—in time—simply slip from memory. She had taken the mementos of David—the photographs and letters sent by friends to make a Book of Remembrance—and put them all away in a box under the bed to be dealt with at a later date.

"I suppose I was torn between the sadness that they might forget and the fear that they might remember and pine. I decided to take my lead from them. If they didn't want to discuss it, I wasn't going to foist it on them. Children are great survivors, I thought. They *will* come through this if I just give them the space to process it all in their own way."

Now she wondered if she hadn't simply constructed the

flimsiest of self-deceptions; for the truth was that Dan's suppression of his feelings had in effect suited her—had been one less thing to have to deal with. Just getting up and getting dressed had been such a monumental act of will in those early months. She addressed this last directly to me, as if making an appeal for clemency. "Unless you've been through it, it's impossible to imagine how all-consuming, how draining grief can be."

Much of the literature she had read on her Internet trawl addressed the fact that the children who fared best after losing a parent were those who had been helped to find the appropriate language to frame their feelings. More alarmingly still, she had learned that children of the age Dan then was tend to use their own systems of logic to make sense of the event and can become convinced—unless reassured otherwise—that they had in some way caused the death.

"And then a really strange thought occurred to me." She waited, as if for me to ready myself. "I suddenly wondered if that little D he tattooed on his hand stood not for Dan after all, but for David—or even *Dad*."

My eyes never left her, watching her now rising in distress to begin clearing away the breakfast she had scarcely touched. I couldn't help but admire, despite the solemnity of the conversation, the slim elegance of her form as she moved about the kitchen. She pushed a stray lock of hair behind her ear, and stood so motionless at the window for a moment she might have been a figure in a Holbein painting.

"When I look back, it's so obvious that the roots of Dan's troubles can be traced to that time. There was never anything you could put your finger on. Just that slightly withdrawn, solitary quality he had. I remember his form teacher at the time suggesting a bereavement counselor. I did take him, but it wasn't a huge success. The counselor said that perhaps it was still too early—that I should try again in a few months. And somehow I never got round to it. You know, little by little, life resumed. The grief began to feel more manageable. I suppose I just instinctively decided to let go, to concentrate on moving forward. And then of course, I met you."

Annie sat down again and propped her face on her hands. I could see the legacy of the late night in her dark eyes, but exhaustion had also lent her face a luminous quality, and a tenderness rose in me. She was propelled by such quiet determination.

"Maybe when you came along it only intensified all these unresolved feelings inside him. And when we told him we were going to get married, perhaps he felt the only solution to the inner turmoil it triggered in him was to physically remove himself. To run away."

These days the Internet made armchair experts of us all, I reflected, though outwardly I was nodding as if in thoughtful accord. The mystery of Dan's disappearance left a void the imagination was compelled to fill. I could hardly begrudge Annie the comfort of a narrative. And she had alighted on one that so neatly corresponded with one of the central orthodoxies of our times—that our behavior and choices are often motivated by repressed impulses that we must lay bare if we are to discover the essential truth about ourselves—a belief so ubiquitous it had become conflated with fact.

"In a funny kind of way, I feel relieved. For the first time I can begin to relate to what it was that might have been troubling him. Maybe even to empathize a bit with why he might have felt compelled to go. And though it's terrifying to think of him out there somewhere on his own, I try to take comfort in the fact that he's quite a streetwise child. That's one thing at least I suppose that terrible school gave him. Perhaps he's found somewhere to lie low for a while. I mean, you might think I'm grasping at straws, but you must admit it's possible. In time he could come to see things differently, and feel ready to come home again."

She touched her fingertips together as if she had shared something extremely private and precious. I couldn't help but be heartened by this glimmer of a revival. Faith was restoring her beauty again. Though it did indeed strike me that she was grasping at straws, it would cost me nothing to keep my own counsel. For the time being at least.

20

Fortified by this new theory, Annie now set about trying to discover where a child who had run away might secrete himself. Her first move was to try to contact the only refuge that actually housed runaways. Though its telephone number and location were a well-kept secret, through sheer dint of perseverance, together with help from a sympathetic man from the NSPCC, she eventually managed to speak to someone who worked there. But the voice on the other end of the phone said that a visit would be out of the question. They were strictly forbidden to reveal not only the location of the refuge, but even the names of any children staying there. They explained that their role was to protect young people from organized crime and sexual exploitation, which all too often meant having to shield them from their own parents. So though they had every sympathy for her situation, they could only assure her that they maintained certain lines of communication with the police and advise that she continue to cooperate with the ongoing police investigation.

For a while Annie lost heart again. She said she couldn't help but resent this faceless professional who had closed ranks against her. I suppose too, the suggestion that Dan might, if only by implication, be in need of protection from his own mother chimed all too painfully with the burden of guilt and self-recrimination she already carried. It wasn't long though before she rallied and began to contact other organizations for runaways she found on her Internet trawls. But though she was greeted everywhere with sympathy, she found no one who could offer any new insights or practical help. And on one fundamental point they all concurred. A child who didn't want to be found could remain missing indefinitely.

More than once, Annie took me with her on late-night searches through Paddington and King's Cross, and we cruised the darkened streets, craning our heads this way and that to scan the passersby. It was summer by now, and a new record-breaking heatwave had unleashed a sensual festivity. The slipstreams of warm air passing continually through our open car windows carried vivid gusts of perfume and tobacco, or sometimes a pungent drain. All races and nations were to be found on the streets of London, congregating in the numerous cafés and restaurants, or strolling the night streets in animated conversation.

An almost missionary zeal appeared to possess Annie as she gripped the steering wheel, scanning this way and that.

It took a while to spot the potential runaways who flashed into sight at the curbside, wan-faced teenagers keeping a nervy eye out for potential drug dealers or punters.

Despite myself, I was carried on her faith. It is impossible to describe the sensation we both shared on these trips. The tantalizing possibility that we might turn a corner and there, at long last, would be Dan! Together with a concurrent dread at the prospect of finding him, fallen among thieves and prostitutes, degraded beyond redemption.

"Look! Over there!" she would sometimes cry, urgently gesturing. And we would both crane our heads, straining to get a better look at the latest fair-haired boy she had spotted. Yet the face when they turned was always that of a stranger. And as we glided past, the heart pounding would subside into hollow anti-climax.

It takes a while to scroll through the pictures on the missing children's Web site. I stood beside Annie one day, watching over her shoulder as she scanned through. Outside, the heatwave continued. The meadows were full of children playing ball games and scantily clad adults sunning themselves, while their dogs flopped beside them with lolling tongues, like comedy drunks. Yet here was Annie sitting with the blind lowered, at her computer once again.

She showed me some of the stories listed there, each a vignette of disrupted family lives that poignantly echoed our own. Some had been missing for just a short while, others for a matter of years. Here they were, pictured in a carefree unremarkable moment before it all unraveled. Many, perhaps the majority, appeared to have been abducted by a parent in access disputes, or to have an established history of running away. There were only a handful of children whose whereabouts and reason for disappearing—like Dan's—remained a mystery. Annie clicked through the case histories before coming at last to our own. Then she closed the computer down without a word and went upstairs.

Though Angela still came occasionally to see us, we had long since stopped expecting her to bring any news. For by now it was apparent to us both that the police had exhausted all fruitful lines of inquiry. Months had passed, and yet the plain fact of the matter was that we had as little insight into what might have befallen Dan as we did on the day he vanished. We took great care never to actually acknowledge this state of affairs to each other, still less to consider its probable implications. That would have been to break an unspoken rule. Privately, however, I couldn't but brood on it, and so it was that, little by little, I let the dwindling embers of hope go cold.

19

A year's anniversary came and went, marked by a national television appeal, which was met by a resounding silence. A silence that only served to underscore how our lives remained on hold, continually waiting for a resolution that never came. Looking about me at the habitual disorder of the house, I couldn't but observe in dismay how many of the scattered possessions still belonged to Dan. Yet Annie remained adamant that everything should be left just as it was. So Dan's sports bag continued to hang from the coat stand, while his Rollerblades and muddy football boots still lay in a heap underneath, until the day, on an exasperated impulse, I went round and seized everything up, before thrusting it all into the cupboard under the stairs. Though Annie never mentioned it, I tried to convince myself that she might secretly have been relieved.

Even then Dan's old belongings might surface unexpectedly, having lurked in overlooked nooks and crannies, like little booby traps designed to startle us from forgetfulness. One summer's day I came across his muddy Frisbee lodged in the tangled depths of the hedge. I rinsed it under the tap, thinking I would show it to Annie before changing my mind and putting it away with all the other things under the stairs.

Not long afterwards I found her staring sorrowfully at something she held cupped like treasure in her hands. She showed me a silver harmonica she had just retrieved from behind the cushion pads of the sofa, together with a tattered slip of paper. She had given the harmonica to Dan in his last Christmas stocking, she said.

When she smoothed the piece of paper flat, I saw that Dan had been practizing the tag name *Zeus!* in that looping hand one sees anointing so many public walls now. "I used to see the name written in quite a few places round here," she said, "but it never occurred to me to make the connection with Dan." I suppose in different circumstances it might have afforded me some wry amusement to discover that the gift of the *Iliad* had not fallen entirely on barren ground after all.

It was, I think I'm right in saying, around the second anniversary of Dan's disappearance that Annie sank into depression again. Then for days the fridge was bereft of food, and the lone pint of milk there rancid, while her college work went unmarked. In the mornings she would dress for work straight from the laundry basket, wearily pulling out the wrinkled clothes she found there, apparently hoping that a brisk shake would be enough to render them fresh and ready to be worn again. Meanwhile the contents of the house appeared to have been newly spun about by a hurricane passing wildly on its way.

During this period, she spent most weekends sleeping for hours at a time, rather as if some sustaining cog in the mechanism had simply ceased to turn. It had been a while since her GP helped wean her off the antidepressants that had helped see her through the first year, so it was with some alarm that I discovered she was now buying both Valium and sleeping tablets illegally on the Internet.

In an attempt to rouse herself, Annie sat down with Rachel one day to assemble a collage of family photographs in a framed display case. Once they had finished, I hung it above Rachel's bed, and the three of us stood back to admire their handiwork. Dan, of course, featured prominently in almost every picture, and Annie stood ruminating on the images for some moments before turning to put her arms around Rachel.

"You've waited so patiently, darling. Surely—*surely* it can't be much longer now."

I heard this with a sinking heart. Though negotiations to establish common ground between a believer and a skeptic are inevitably delicate, I resolved that for Rachel's sake the time had come to take a stand. I could no longer ignore the fact that my restraint had become an unwitting collusion.

"I can't help wondering if it isn't a little unwise to give Rachel such a definite impression of Dan waiting in the wings like that," I said in a conversational tone to Annie, later that night. She was crouched in front of the washing machine unloading a basket of clothes, and I noted uneasily how her busy hands at once froze midway between basket and machine.

"Oh really! In what way might it be unwise?"

"Well, I suppose it raises expectations that may never actually be fulfilled. That's all."

The silence that opened between us was so fraught it seemed hardly a silence at all. She glanced sharply at me before resuming her work. It was extraordinary how I had only to touch on the subject for the very air to chill between us.

"Wouldn't it be better to make it clear that we simply don't know?" I chose my words with care, for I skated right at the raw nub of her now. Yet her expression remained masklike. She picked up the laundry basket.

"Fine. If that's what you prefer."

It was a victory of sorts, and yet it didn't feel like one. For the rest of the evening we evaded each other's eyes, exchanging occasional bright remarks in a strained tone, and once or twice I heard her hum with such affected carelessness when I passed that I shrank inwardly.

After that, though she was careful never to make any further references to Dan in my presence, I couldn't help but wonder what was said in my absence. I, for my part, took care to remain scrupulously impartial whenever his name came up, though it is possible my exclusive use of the past tense may have hinted at my true view. Typically, Rachel, with her innate diplomacy, betrayed no sign of whose side she might incline to.

Having once been entirely open about her body, Annie took to locking the door when she bathed. Undressing for bed became a hasty and furtive disrobing; the lovely curve of her back, the glimpsed side globe of breast frequently leaving me wracked by desire long after she had put out the light and slipped into sleep. Our increasingly intermittent love-making was something she appeared more to tolerate than participate in. In the face of which, a self-loathing grew in me—that I should have become yet another thing in her life to be endured. Eventually, I could no longer bear to initiate anything, and the sexual aspect of our relationship simply dwindled away.

A mother's tenacity is an extraordinary thing. Three presents for each missed birthday, and another three for each missed Christmas now sat wrapped and waiting on the top shelf of the wardrobe in Dan's bedroom. As his thirteenth birthday approached, not long after his disappearance, she had been adamant that we mark it. If he were to return, it was important he should know that he had never been far from our thoughts.

Three months later, when December came, she used the same argument to set a Christmas present aside for him.

The next year, as Dan's fourteenth birthday loomed into view, she made no reference to the date, and I allowed myself to hope that this time she would allow it to pass unmarked. Yet when I opened the cupboard the next day to double-check, I found to my dismay a second birthday present—*For darling Dan.*

Then, three months later, on the shelf next to it, another Christmas present: *I miss you more than I can say.*

When the third year came, the same scenario was repeated. No references of any kind as the day approached, no mention of anything on the day itself. Once again, I was compulsively drawn by a sense of foreboding to the cupboard. Once again, first the birthday present: *No one to cry for, live for, love.* She had evidently been reading my collection of Pushkin. Then three months later, another for Christmas. This time I found she had plundered Tennyson. *I hold it true, what'er befall; I feel it, when I sorrow most; 'Tis better to have loved and lost, Than never to have loved at all.*

Though she indignantly denied it on the one occasion I was bold enough to ask, I suspected that she made regular pilgrimages to Dan's room at the top of the house. Certainly, despite the passage of years, it remained exactly as he had left it. A profusion of posters covered its two sloping walls, dominated by a quasi-religious image of one of his gangster heroes, whose eyes were fixed skywards like some latter-day muscle-bound Messiah. The bed was made in readiness, with the wrap Dan had bought from Camden

Market draped across it, and his teddy bear tucked under the counterpane, its worn head resting on the pillow as if in lieu of Dan himself.

The drawers retained their trove of boyish treasures—in one a collection of mysteriously sourced penknives and lighters, in another an assortment of bangers and stink bombs. While on the floor stood the glass tank that housed Chip the gecko, a creature who had revealed himself to have prodigious powers of endurance. For in the early days of Dan's disappearance, Annie had forgotten all about him, only to recall his existence with a guilty start when she happened to notice a movement in his cage some months later. Mortified at her inadvertent neglect, she had hastened to the pet shop to buy the live crickets she remembered Dan feeding him. One of the stories Rachel often begged to hear retold was the time Dan brought home a box of newly purchased crickets from the pet shop, only to stumble and drop it in the hall. Though he assured Annie he had successfully recaptured all of them, for months afterwards a full-throated chirruping would start up from behind the radiators every time the heating came on—just as if a blazing Mediterranean summer day were dawning.

Now and then I would tentatively raise the possibility of rehousing Chip. It was a circuitous way of testing the waters, I suppose—of obliquely assessing without confrontation how far along the path of letting go Annie had progressed. Each time I hoped that she would finally agree, with a regretful shrug, that yes, perhaps it was for the best. It would be the first concrete sign that this limbo we inhabited was at last drawing to a conclusion—that we could begin to take up the threads of our old life again, to make plans, to move forward. Yet each time her fierce refusal to even contemplate such a possibility made it perfectly plain that any such acceptance still remained a far distant prospect.

On a number of occasions, Annie reported seeing a boy getting on a bus, or disappearing into a shop, who looked so like Dan her heart had leaped into her mouth. Though she would almost instantly realize her mistake, the lancing sensation of renewed loss would take some while to recede. These ghostly sightings were a curious phenomenon, as if, unable to process Dan's absence, the mind simply resurrected its own version of him, randomly superimposing it like a hologram onto passersby.

Once she had actually given chase. A traveling steam fair had pitched camp one Easter holiday, and after much nagging, Rachel had persuaded Annie to take her. As she stood watching Rachel enjoying the ride, she couldn't help but be reminded how much Dan had once loved their trips to the fair too. *And I always gave you such a hard time about the expense of it all,* she thought regretfully, waving and smiling at Rachel as she spun past. *I can't imagine now how I ever found it in me to begrudge you anything.* No sooner had she thought this, than Dan unexpectedly appeared from nowhere, striding boldly through the press of people. That distinctive loping gait. The profile so instantly recognizable, she cried out in amazement.

Seeing that he was about to vanish among the crowds, she seized Rachel's hand as she disembarked from her ride and set off in determined pursuit, nimbly maneuvering through the mass of people who thronged their way. As she ran, she attempted to call his name, only to find that shock had literally rendered her dumb. Still no words came as hard on his heels they skirted the bumper cars, colliding with a rotund woman who squawked in alarm, before they at last succeeded in drawing abreast of him.

"*Please!*" she managed, reaching out to grasp his shoulder, and at last he turned—to reveal features that bore no resemblance of any kind to Dan's. A spiteful face, the shifty eyes set too close together. It had been like a knife going through her to see the chimera dissolve in an instant, spirited away by the revelation of this stranger. She had gawped at him in wordless horror, before shrinking back, drawing Rachel with her.

Walking home from the station late one night, with a drink or two inside me, I passed the allotments and inhaled the fragrance of cut grass, the first of the year, and a rush of well-being arose in me. With it came a sentimental throb of feeling for Annie quite as sharp and vital as when we first met. Whatever had become of our wedding plans, I wondered, the light restlessness of the air making it seem that I glided home on skates. High time we patched things up, I thought, astonished at how straightforward a task it suddenly appeared. It was as if the sweet peppery aroma of the grass had lit up new pathways of possibility. These difficulties, these failures of communication crept up so slowly that one submitted to them without even realizing how much of value had been conceded. I turned into the close. Wasn't it up to me to prompt regeneration just as determinedly as the gardener must water his crop?

As I opened the front door it was as if it gave way onto this bright new chapter about to open between us. Hadn't Annie sometimes complained I wouldn't talk about things? Well, we would talk. Tonight we would talk.

The ground floor was in darkness but upstairs a light still blazed, and I mounted the stairs with rising ardor. I found Annie in the bathroom, cleaning her teeth.

"Darling!"

"Hey."

Already she was turning away, but I caught her about the waist, smiling at her pale reflection in the mirror. She leaned forward to spit into the sink, before securing her dressing gown more tightly. Her narrowed eyes met mine in the mirror.

"Don't, Julian. Please. I'm really not in the mood."

She put the toothbrush away and dried her mouth on the corner of the towel like a diner who has finished her meal.

"I've taken a sleeping tablet and I'm going to go to bed now," she said, with such decisiveness the last remnants of optimism slipped from me.

She walked into the bedroom and stood at the foot of the bed. "Today was about as bad a day as I can remember."

"I've been thinking the two of us should go away somewhere. Take a holiday."

She sighed one of her heartfelt sighs.

"You know perfectly well I couldn't leave the house empty for that long."

I remembered why I avoided these conversations now. How little I cared for this otherworldly martyred voice she assumed. She might be auditioning for the part of Ophelia, I thought with a flash of savage spite. All she lacked was a torn dress, and a bunch of dying flowers. I stepped towards her. I don't know what it was I had in mind. One last impetuous attempt to take her in my arms—to get her despite everything to yield—but she only shook her head sadly, as if I too were a matter of regret, and, brushing past me, climbed into bed.

"You've been drinking," she said, as she switched the light off. I hadn't known darkness could fall like a blow. It was a moment before I managed to gather myself. I went downstairs and poured myself another drink, before making up a bed on the sofa.

In this way, we lived side by side—and yet apart. My willingness to endure this state of affairs might perhaps perplex you, yet in truth a fatal yearning for that which is out of reach has proved a marked and lifelong trait in me. I can see now that the further she withdrew, the more I came to idealize her. Indeed, it was this trait that was to prove my eventual undoing. In the immortal words of so many popular songs, you might be forgiven for concluding, I was a fool for love.

18

Despite the fact that I never particularly wanted a child of my own, in time I had come to feel like Rachel's father in every way but blood. As I told Stanley in our first interview, I had always been disarmed by the touching way in which she welcomed me into the family and from the outset found her a charmingly old-fashioned child, demure in her manners and eager to please.

The year I moved in with Annie was the year Rachel, aged no more than four, sang a solo at the local primary school's Christmas concert, revealing a voice of such purity it delighted all who heard it. I often persuaded her to sing for me after that, and there were times when she did that I found myself deeply moved.

Rachel loved to hear stories from my own childhood, in particular from my years at boarding school. The day of my arrival there at the tender age of seven. My subsequent wily attempts to outwit the sadomasochistic attentions of an older boy with a penchant for staging mock executions and locking small boys in chests. Or the saga that led to the scar on my arm (the legacy of an accidentally self-inflicted injury caused by a forbidden penknife that then became a festering wound and had to be kept hidden from the masters), all became favorite and oft-repeated tales. I liked to believe they would provide inspirational examples of my early independence. For it has always been my sincere belief that it was this self-reliance cultivated in me at an early age that has proved my greatest ally in life.

As Rachel grew older, I found myself struck by the way in which her childish utterances so often contained—to the discerning listener at least—a profundity that belied her years. Annie worried that her consistently high grades and unfailing helpfulness were an unconscious attempt to compensate us for the loss of her brother—and looking back, it is possible that there was something in this. Certainly I can't deny that now her mother was so often subdued and lost to melancholy, Rachel's youthful high spirits had become, with each passing year, a source of great solace to me. We would often escape the oppressive solemnity of the house together, to roam the vast expanse of fields on every side. We might visit the play park, a shabby concreted area that appeared to have dropped out of the sky to fall randomly at the edge of the meadows, or join the towpath that ran for miles along the northern bank of the Thames.

Annie's quiet cul de sac of privately owned homes was something of an anomaly in the area, nestled as it was among some of the borough's less salubrious council estates. Her house was one of the twelve postwar pebble-dashed dwellings that adjoined the great grassy area known as Fishers Meadows. In effect Fishers Meadows was a quite distinct kingdom, bordered along three of its sides by the oxbow of the river—and it was as if only the city at its peripheries had moved forward, leaving this pocket of land untouched by time, with the river embracing it like a moat.

On summer evenings, dogwalkers and runners would crisscross the meadows, while Middle Eastern families might gather with barbecues and hookah pipes to picnic under the trees. The thump of music from the open windows of the Fishers Estate could frequently be heard drifting out across the bleak courtyards where children swarmed in play. Hooded boys from the estate were often to be seen wheeling up and down the through road on bicycles, like diminutive vigilantes patrolling their turf. Meanwhile their older counterparts—now barrel-chested men—would swagger down the excrement-fouled alleyway and out onto the meadows beyond, tugged by their muscle-bound fighting dogs. This was the estate where the local council housed difficult families and asylum seekers, a combustible combination that meant it was not uncommon to see police cars gliding in and out. Conversely, there was always a steady flow of four-by-fours cruising the winding road that crossed the playing fields, bearing mothers and nannies to the private health club at the far outskirts of the meadows, where their golden-haired progeny could be coached in tennis or tai kwon do.

Though initially I had rather despised Fishers Meadows as a shabby backwater, in time I came not only to relish its social diversity, but to see it as a forum for all kinds of quietly surreal events. In the early days of our courtship I had been astonished to see a hundred or so jewel-green parakeets clustering noisily in one of the trees. Annie had explained that though no one knew where the birds originated from, they now flew in great flocks about the area. On another occasion as I strolled along, a car drew to a halt under the lime trees. The driver and passenger, both perfectly unremarkable-looking middle-aged men, got out and together strolled to the back of the car, whereupon one opened up the boot and helped the other climb in before slamming it closed and driving away. I took particular pleasure in the nun I sometimes glimpsed in the distance, whisking along the towpath with her wimple flying about her in the wind.

In time, at Rachel's prompting, a game evolved in which, when we stepped out of the front door, it was as if into an enchanted land. I would point out the crescent-shaped indentations of horses' hooves in the turf that so often puzzled me—for I had never in all the times I walked there actually set eyes on a rider and horse—and we would entertain each other with stories of the phantom horseman who roamed the meadows while we slept.

My most uplifting moments, however, came when I walked here alone. For it was then that I could truly revel in the vast space that opened about me as I rounded the end of Annie's close, the city no more than a distant haze along the horizon. Dwarfed by the great bowl of sky, my eye would be drawn upwards to the immense canvas of changing cloudscapes. Flocks of birds passed in every direction overhead, their trajectories often crossing with the planes on their diagonal journey to or from Heathrow. And this constant transit of bird and plane, the ever-changing arrangements of cloud and sky color, all served to remind me of how insubstantial so many of my troubles were. I often thought with feeling of Ruskin when he regretted man's failure to attend to the sky as I walked with my head tilted heavenwards.

There is a sweet nostalgia in such memories. Together with a melancholy that I was able to lose myself for so long in such comforting abstractions. For the truth was that Annie and I might have been passengers aboard the *Titanic*, borne by inexorable tides towards the extraordinary event that would, before the year was out, change everything.

17

One day, as we drew to the end of that third year, Annie came home in a state of dazed agitation. She held a cluster of carrier bags filled with heavy groceries in each hand, and let their weight fall from her before sinking slowly into a chair as I hastened forward in alarm. She said that a young man had stopped her in the supermarket, greeting her by name with a broad smile. At first she hadn't the least idea who he might be. He certainly wasn't one of her old students; she had been quite certain of that. She would have continued on her way, but his manner was so self-assured she was forced to politely confess her bewilderment.

"I used to live on the Fishers Estate," he said. "Dan and me was in the same class at school. I'm Amman! Amman Kazi."

At this, her puzzlement only deepened. She remembered Amman Kazi perfectly well. A bright-eyed, rather sweet-faced little boy. Yet here before her stood a tall, broad-chested young man. Then –

"Amman!" she exclaimed, stepping back in wonder as the penny finally dropped, the boy she remembered and this young man before her clicking together as one. "Of course I remember you. Amman Kazi!"

A statuesque nose had sprouted, dwarfing the bright eyes and merry smile. Though as she scrutinized him she saw how the eyes still retained the ghost of the child she remembered. She'd had to stop herself from exclaiming at how he'd grown, knowing it to be the standard platitude of all adults when confronted with a child they'd not seen for some while. But the trouble was, she could think of nothing else to offer, her mind still reeling at the transformation.

"You must be doing your GCSEs now?" she managed at last.

He nodded, grimacing. "Can't wait for it all to end. To get on with real life."

"What will you do?"

"Nothing. Sweet FA." Once again, that bold smile.

"Amman," she said again, aware of a renewed sorrow shifting within her as she scanned his face.

"I often think of Dan, you know," he said, seeming to intuit her thoughts and sounding sincerely regretful. "It was a very sad thing that. Very sad indeed. Me mum was well gutted. She never let me take the bus to school afterwards. I had to wait behind for me uncle to come and get me."

Annie had never considered how the reverberations

would have rippled out through the community, altering lives beyond our own. That in itself was a surprise. But what really shocked her, she said, was the realization that Dan too must now be a young man. In her mind's eye she had entirely failed to allow for this, each birthday when it came serving only as an abstract reminder of time's passage.

That night she cried for the first time in a long while. He had still been so very much a child when he went. Only the most fleeting signs had hinted at any changes stirring within him. Once or twice after he had come in from playing football, she had caught the startling onion smell of perspiration. In addition to which, he had become unexpectedly modest around her in that last year. Initially, this had disconcerted her, since as a family they had always walked in an unselfconscious state of undress about the house. But then an attendant discomfort rose in her, and she took to covering her own nakedness when he was around. It had seemed absurd when he was still so physically undeveloped. Yet the changes puberty would bring were already manifesting themselves among many of his classmates. The day she'd spotted Dan and Obi coming out of school and pulled over to offer them a lift, she couldn't help but be struck by the discrepancy in their height and build as she drew alongside them. Afterwards she had wondered whether that might not be one of the reasons Dan strove to put on a display of such exaggerated machismo.

"What about that time," I reminded her, "you found that rather dog-eared pornography magazine in his school bag?"

She laughed out loud, clapping a hand to her mouth and exclaiming that she had completely forgotten it. My advice had been to simply replace it and say nothing, but after careful thought she decided instead to throw it away. When Dan got home, she told him of her discovery quite casually.

"Wasn't mine," he muttered at once, flushing scarlet, "Obi give it me. Said his cousin stole it." He was pivoting restlessly towards the door, as if longing to propel himself through it.

"I'm not asking where you got it, and I'm not cross with you for having it. It's perfectly normal to be curious. But I do think there are more appropriate ways for you to learn about these things . . . And if there's anything you want to clarify—anything that puzzles or worries you—you'll find me surprisingly unshockable on the subject of sex."

He had by now pulled his head so deep into his collar, it was as if, finding all other exits barred to him, his only hope was to retract into his clothing like a tortoise. When Annie reported the conversation to me afterwards, I recalled precisely the same reaction as a schoolboy—any discourse with an adult on such matters creating a sensation of mortification so acute it actually deafened you, as if cymbals were clashing in your ears.

We were both laughing now, and when Annie got to her feet I was greatly relieved to see her mood so much improved.

Afterwards it occurred to me that it was the first time I had heard her speak of Dan with anything other than melancholy. And I saw how fortuitous the encounter with Amman had been. For it had evidently crystallized just how much time had now passed. I realized that it probably wouldn't take much encouragement to coax her into at last drawing her long vigil to its inevitable if heartbreaking conclusion.

Over the past three years I had formed my own theory about Dan's disappearance. I thought that in all probability he had taken off after school on his bicycle that day, thinking he would visit the high street for a bit. Perhaps, as Annie and the police surmised, he was angry about our wedding plans. Or perhaps it was simply an impulsive bid for adventure. But somehow, somewhere on that ill-fated journey, he had fallen into bad company. Met with some kind of . . . Here my thoughts always reeled queasily away. It wasn't necessary to pursue the details. It was enough to face the fact that something terrible and untoward had obviously occurred. And though it wasn't a theory I felt I could ever share with Annie, it nonetheless offered a rationale that now shored up my resolve.

At first I tried various circumspect means of broaching the issue, yet she was resolute in refusing to pick up on any of my cautious overtures. And each time I had to overcome a deep aversion to actually articulating the subject we had for so long tiptoed around. But eventually I took myself in hand by preparing in advance a little speech, which I delivered one evening before my courage could fail me.

"I wonder whether the time hasn't come to think about holding some kind of simple ceremony for Dan. I've often thought of what you told me about the importance of funerals. It would be a chance to say good-bye. At the very least, you owe that to Rachel. Perhaps we might even have a think about clearing out his room."

Annie gazed at me for some time without uttering a word. I had never seen her so pale.

"How eager you are to write him off," she muttered in a faraway voice. "It's quite extraordinary." Her eyes drifted to the window where a murky twilight was swiftly falling upon the street. Then she turned to me with the oddest expression. "You never cared for him much, did you? I used to try and make excuses for you by reminding myself you hadn't spent much time with children. But it wasn't that. It couldn't have been, since you always made such a favorite of Rachel. There was just something about him you could never seem to reconcile yourself to."

I suppose it was the injustice of this personal attack that made me harden my heart, bringing us to a most regrettable turning point.

"Now look, Annie. I really don't think we can fudge this any longer. The plain fact of the matter is that it has been three years now. Three years without a single sighting of Dan. Three years without a single word or sign to suggest that there is even the slightest reason for optimism. In all likelihood we will never know what has become of him—and God knows, that's pretty rough on you. But I'm afraid the time has come to take stock. Surely you can see how this refusal to face facts prevents you from moving forward?

If we're ever to have any chance of a proper life together, we must, for both our sakes, draw a line under the past now."

Her agitated fingers had found a thread of cotton trailing from her hem.

"I've never said this before," she murmured, the hem unraveling as she spoke. "I suppose it's something I've tried not to admit even to myself. But ask yourself this, Julian. Has it never occurred to you that it was your inexplicable hostility towards my son that made him run away?"

Then she rose with great dignity, though her dress now hung lopsided, and left the room.

The next evening, I came home from work to find the locks changed and all my belongings in bin liners outside the front door. As I stood in some bewilderment, wondering what to do next, I turned to find a dignified and elderly Sikh neighbor I dimly recognized, standing beside me. He was smiling with concern as he looked first at me and then the bags, taking stock of my situation.

"Oh dear, oh dear, oh dear," he offered, patting my arm and glancing towards the house. "The wife is not happy."

I found I still had the front door key at the ready in one hand, and after a moment I put it back in my pocket before turning to survey the bags again. "No, I think we can safely agree that the wife is definitely *not* happy."

"I am on my way to the shops. Perhaps I can give you a lift somewhere?"

I nodded, and he began to load everything into the boot of his car before getting in himself and indicating that I was to take the passenger seat beside him, his manner so quietly commanding, I found I was grateful to submit. He knew of a nice place, he told me as we set off, and he would take me there without further ado. After a short while we drew alongside a dilapidated row of buildings and stopped outside Bhopinder's Bed & Breakfast. As he unloaded everything again, he explained in a manner now tempered by something rather more businesslike, that the hotel was owned by one of his cousins who he was sure could be persuaded to offer me a very favorable rate. It was there that I stayed while I tried to work out my next move.

16

Still feeling shell-shocked, I decided to take a shabby studio flat in Shepherd's Bush as a temporary stopgap. Though a colleague had offered to loan me a rather more well-appointed flat in Marylebone, I couldn't face being so far from Rachel and Annie. I learned later that Rachel had wept bitterly when Annie broke the news to her, and was placated only when her mother agreed I might come on Saturday mornings to take her out for an hour or two. It was this slender connection alone that sustained me. "I still believe we can make this work," I told Annie when she called to discuss the arrangements. "I only hope that in time you will reconsider."

It was the end of summer, and a clammy humidity thickened the air. A plague of daddy longlegs danced about my dismal new flat, rising and falling like a mutant uprising of airborne spiders. Housed in a 1930s mansion block, it was a charmless space, furnished with cheap MDF fittings that continually came apart at the seams, marked and scuffed by the wretched down-on-their-luck tenants I imagined had preceded me. It was here that I brooded on Annie's accusation, endlessly improving the replies I should have offered in my defense, though the truth was that I was smarting from a feeling that she had located a nerve as deep and hidden as coal. Despite this, I continued to work assiduously on my defense. Yes, it was perfectly true that Dan had been an enigma to me. And yes, perhaps there were times when his oafish manners had grated. But in the main, my strategy—inasmuch as I had pursued one—had been to stand back and leave them to it. Indeed, their relationship appeared so impenetrable it left me little choice. Evidently, Annie had mistaken my restraint for something rather more malign. I felt it a bitter pill that it should be this forbearance that now so damned me in her eyes.

As I said at the beginning, the view backwards sometimes affords unexpected new perspectives. Quite unbidden, small instances now sidled crablike from dark recesses of the memory, as if offering themselves up to me for reappraisal. There had been that evening, for example, a few months before Dan disappeared, when he had hung about me with a shiftiness I simply presumed was a precursor to one of his mumbled requests for money. When I finally asked in exasperation if he hadn't any homework he should be doing, he muttered something about a football match he was playing the following weekend. "You can come and watch if you like," I remembered his saying in a studiedly offhand tone. I think I briskly promised to do my best before shooing him from the room. And somehow I never actually made it. I can't remember why now—circumstances conspired—something came up. In truth, I have never had much appetite for competitive sport. Yet for some reason I assumed no explanation or apology to be necessary, and neither of us ever referred to the matter again. Now I wondered uneasily whether Dan might have scanned the sidelines hopefully before turning away crestfallen. For the first time it occurred to me that the invitation had been an olive branch of sorts—and that my failure to respond in kind might well have wounded him.

This growing unease soon tainted my dreams too. One night I drifted off to sleep to find a door springing open on a room whose shadowy interior I somehow knew would contain something reprehensible. In the dream I was back once again in Fishers Meadows. It was nighttime, and a breeze came through the open windows of the bedroom, causing the curtains to billow inwards. At the center of the room lay Annie and me, lost in the throes of lovemaking. With the omniscience of the dreamer I saw Dan in his pajamas passing by our door. He was barely awake, stumbling in the darkness on his way to the bathroom. Yet Annie, lost in her own rising climax, remained entirely oblivious to his passing, and instead of hushing her moans as I knew I should, I chose instead to urge her on—thinking it no bad thing the boy should grasp the carnal bonds that bound us.

Then abruptly I was awake again and sitting up in bed, drenched in sweat, finding myself back in the dismal flat, with only the noise of the night buses passing along the main road for company.

There were other dreams too, dreams in which I chased him through the house and out into the street. Even when I awoke I would still retain an impression of his fists pounding at the door, his contorted face pressed imploringly at the window. More disturbingly still, the face was sometimes that of David, Dan's dead father! Living, raging in my head just as vividly as if I had known him in life.

Though I have never set any store by dreams, knowing perfectly well that they are no more than the random shiftings of the mind, very soon I came to dread bedtimes and the disturbing nocturnal landscape that awaited me once sleep came. Eventually, I sought comfort by resurrecting a childhood habit first discovered in my dormitory days as a means of quelling homesickness, and took to sleeping with a radio under my pillow, keeping the volume so low it was no more than a comforting murmur in my ear.

For reasons I couldn't quite account for, I had hit a losing streak, and things rapidly went from bad to worse. Hastening between meetings in Mayfair a few days later, I was hailed from across Grosvenor Square by Francis Benson, an old client whose family owned several galleries on Bond Street.

"Do you remember going to that auction house in Stroud to cast an eye over that painting for me?" he asked, bearing down on me through the traffic with a wrathful expression, apparently deaf to the protesting hoots of cars as they slowed to let him pass.

"Yes," I said, somewhat taken aback at his belligerent tone. "Of course I do. Bellow, Boyd and Willoughby's."

"Do you recall assuring me," he went on, now standing over me in a distinctly menacing manner, "that the painting was not, as I had suspected and hoped, an unattributed portrait by Lorenzo Lotto, but only a later and rather undistinguished copy?"

I nodded with a sense of rising doom.

"Well, you might like to know that the dealer who bought it there for a pittance just sold it for two million. So it was an original, after all. Evidently you are a complete charlatan—though I can't say I wasn't warned. Your reputation is at best checkered. And perhaps I can only blame myself for not listening. You can rest assured, however, that I will be making it my business to let the story be known about town."

Then he turned on his heel and strode away. This would have been sickening enough news at any time. But in the midst of my current woes, I hadn't the resources. I nipped into the Audley for a quick pick-me-up, and it was some hours later before I was ready to emerge again.

It was this melancholy state of affairs that formed the background to a regrettable episode that occurred on a business trip to Brussels a few days later. An episode I recall even now with some hesitation, principally because it offers an uncomfortable measure of how far my life had by then unraveled. Sitting dejectedly in the bar of the hotel just off the Grand Place, I gave scant attention to the arrival of an unaccompanied woman, though I could see in the mirror that we sat like bookends at either end of the long bar. I was somewhat startled therefore, when she appeared unexpectedly at my elbow and, pointing at the empty stool beside me, boldly asked if she might join me.

"Please do," I said, springing to my feet in a belated attempt to cover the surprise all too visible on my face.

"So you are English . . ." She arranged herself on the stool with casual elegance, throwing her head back to blow an aristocratic plume of cigarette smoke at the ceiling. "And evidently of the old-school variety." She was smiling mischievously, her short hair and arched eyebrows lending her a strikingly elfin countenance. From the faint trace of an accent I presumed she must be Scandinavian and judged her to be a little younger than me, though she was dressed austerely, with a silk scarf draped around her neck.

Common courtesy demanded I offer her a drink, which she accepted with a cool grace. Yet despite my initial reluctance, she soon proved herself an engaging companion: quick-witted and well informed. I learned that she was a professor of media studies at the University of Copenhagen and only passing through Brussels on business. Somehow we chanced upon a mutual admiration for the films of Aki Kaurismäki. Neither of us referred to our personal lives, though I gathered by implication that her professional life had been nomadic and that she had formed no significant ties. She appeared not to have the least interest in my own situation, and as I lost track of the rounds, a pleasant camaraderie soon crept upon the proceedings; a rather wittier and more expansive persona slowly infusing me, while the spikier aspects of her bearing appeared to soften and recede.

The undeniable sexual frisson that alcohol so often conjures in such circumstances was one I recalled only too well from various casual encounters of this kind in the days before Annie. By midnight we were huddled in rather more intimate proximity as we struggled to make ourselves heard over the animated laughter of the young people who now packed the bar. Afterwards I couldn't recall by what flirtatious negotiations we reached my room. Yet once there her kisses were curiously guarded, as if she swam up from a subterranean place to make cautiously intimate contact. She spent some time dimming the lights before undressing in the bathroom. Through the open door I watched as she paused briefly to contemplate herself in the mirror, pensively tracing the outline of one small breast. It was a tableau Hopper would have relished.

Veiled in the half-light, she stepped out, pausing only to take up the silk scarf she had just discarded from about her neck. Her figure was so wirily androgynous I had to suppress a disconcerting impression, as I took her in my arms, that I in some way embraced myself. Then she proceeded to tie the scarf tightly about my eyes with such speed and dexterity I could only conclude it was an entirely familiar procedure to her, and though considerably alarmed, I made no attempt to prevent her.

In this manner—unseeing, lost in the sensory darkness, curiously, horribly electrified—we made love, after which she untied the scarf and promptly fell asleep. At some point in the early hours of the morning I half woke to find her sitting straight-backed beside the window. She was smoking a cigarette, apparently deep in thought, though the gap in the curtains allowed light to reveal only a fragment of her face, leaving the rest in deep shadow. In the morning, to my intense relief, I woke again to find her gone. No politely tepid exchange of e-mail addresses or strained farewells required.

I might have dreamed the whole encounter, except that when I rose to open the curtains and the room filled with autumn sunshine, my eye fell upon the note she had left on the table. *Drifting Clouds*, it read. I pondered this puzzlingly cryptic message for some time before it eventually came to me in a rush of recollection that it was the name of the Kaurismäki film we had been unable to recall in our inebriated state the night before.

Despite a vicious hangover, I set about packing with my customary care. I have always derived a ritualistic satisfaction in packing and the unique catharsis it affords—that momentary elation that comes upon surveying the room and finding all evidence of oneself erased. But today the ritual only served to reinforce the dispiriting realization that I was back where I had started, once more a lone wolf.

I soon learned, however, that events were about to take a most unexpected turn. I had slunk back to London and was in the midst of unpacking when Annie rang with the news. News so astonishing I had the oddest impression of being deafened by noise before the muffled depths of a bell jar closed over me. I had to ask several times that she repeat herself. That she take a deep breath and *slow down,* so frantic was she, alternately laughing and crying like someone quite demented.

"A social worker has just called me from Scotland!" she wept. "He says that Dan has turned up. That he's alive and well, Julian! Alive and well!"

15

A*live and well! In Scotland!* Even in my initial disorientation, I was already speeding through a checklist of more credible explanations for this outlandish assertion. I wondered, in fact, if this might be the onset of a breakdown. Or whether she could be attempting an extremely ill-considered and bizarre prank. And it was only when I insisted she begin at the beginning that the story started to accrue some kind of plausibility.

"Is that by any chance Annie Wray?" the man had asked, and she had brusquely confirmed it, assuming he must be a cold caller she should quickly dispense with.

"My name is Luke Holland," he said. "I'm a careworker calling from a refuge for homeless children in Glasgow. I have a young lad with me."

"A young lad?"

"Yeah. Looks to me to be about fifteen, at a guess. He's a bit confused, you see—doesn't seem to know either his name or how old he is."

As the potential import of the man's words struck home, it was all she could do to continue to support the weight of the phone in her hand.

"He had your telephone number in his pocket. And I thought you might be able to—"

"Is his hair fair?"

"Fair? Yes. Very."

"Does he . . . does he have a small tattoo on his left hand?"

"A little D. Yes, yes, he does."

At this, Annie fell to her knees, beginning to gabble that the boy was her son—*that he had found her lost son!* She had been searching for him, hoping and praying for this moment for three years. The man had been dumbfounded, she said. It was a moment or two before he could collect himself. But once he had done, he hastened to assure her that apart from his disorientation, Dan appeared in good health.

Luke Holland either ran or worked for the refuge—it was hard to take it all in—but Annie clearly remembered him explaining that Dan had walked in off the street with nothing to identify him but the piece of paper on which was written her name and number.

Had she actually spoken to Dan? I pressed, once my own powers of speech eventually returned.

Yes, she cried. Yes, she had! There had been a pause while the social worker fetched him. Then—"Mum. Can I . . ." his voice a tremulous whisper down the line. "*Can I come home, please?*"

At this, Annie began running around the house with the phone in one hand, seizing up her coat, hunting for her car keys. She was coming at once to collect him, she cried. She would drive through the night. But then Dan was gone again, and Luke Holland was back on the line saying he saw no reason at all why, if they got their skates on, he couldn't ask the police to get Dan on the overnight train to London that very evening. "Just leave it with me," he had concluded in a businesslike tone, and when she tried to scribble down the number he proffered, she found that her hand shook so violently the pen made a little drumbeat against the paper.

As she set the phone down she was trembling from head to toe, as if gripped by a violent fever. Could it *really* be that Dan was alive? And about to return? Had the man actually said something about getting him home by the following morning? *The following morning!*

She had wandered in a daze about the room, she said, before falling to her knees. She heard herself laughing ecstatically, even as her teeth were beginning to chatter and the laughter become a keening. She thought of all the questions she should have thought to ask, if only she'd had her wits about her. She had to press her hands against her mouth to quiet herself, and rose up only to fall again, lurching senselessly about the room before being overtaken by an urgent need to share this extraordinary news.

"You'd better call Angela Kofi," I said several times, for she appeared not to be taking anything in.

"Yes!" Annie said wonderingly. "Angela Kofi . . . Yes! She's not going to believe it, is she? There are so many people I need to call. I actually have no idea where to begin."

"Do you want me to come over, Annie?"

"Yes." She had begun to cry again. "Yes, please come. Come as quickly as you can."

Once the conversation ended I walked about, taking in great lungfuls of air. I paced about the flat before finding myself in the park, where I sat on a bench, shaking my head as waves of wonder and disbelief broke alternately over me. Twice I rose to my feet, only to feel my knees fold under me again. The people strolling past me appeared real enough. The gardens they walked through perfectly authentic. After a while I laughed out loud and bent down to touch the ground. The path was cool to the touch, and left a fine dusting of grit on my fingertips. I could detect nothing that might suggest I was in the grip of a hallucination.

Having calmed myself sufficiently, I set off for Fishers Meadows, while Annie went to collect Rachel from school and break the news. Dear Rachel, who was only eight when Dan went and whose life had been so overshadowed by his absence ever since. If she was surprised to see her mother hovering anxiously at the classroom door, she must have been quite thunderstruck when she heard the news Annie brought. The mystery of her brother's fate had loomed so large over her childhood that it must have seemed rather as if a mythical figure were about to step from the pages of a storybook.

When Annie opened the door to me, my impression was of someone lit from within. She threw her arms about me before cupping my face with her hands and kissing me. "Isn't it the most wonderful, extraordinary thing!" she sang, drawing me into the kitchen. Luke Holland had just called to say that Dan was now safely aboard the overnight train and would be arriving in London early the next morning. He had advised her to prepare for a period of recovery and adjustment, she said, before wishing them both the very best of luck.

Somewhere, both the house phone and her mobile were ringing, and Annie hastened ahead. "Oh God, the phones just haven't stopped."

I leaned in the doorway listening as she retold the news to someone I could only presume from the intimacy of her tone must be her sister. "Yes, yes! I spoke to him, I actually spoke to him," she was saying, "and his voice . . ." Her hand flew to her mouth. "Emma, *his voice has broken!*" Tears were streaming down her cheeks.

The moment she put the phone down, she dashed the tears away with the back of her hand before briskly surveying the room. She had so much to do, she exclaimed with a shaky laugh, that she didn't know quite where to begin. "And it's only twelve hours now! Twelve hours and he'll be home again!"

At once she set forth, bustling to and fro, throwing open

cupboards and bringing out a multitude of ingredients. She had bought chicken Kiev to make a special lunch for him, she explained. The same dish she chose that fateful day three years earlier. And she was going to make an apple crumble. Did I remember how much Dan had always loved apple crumble?

I watched her, delighting in this effervescent creature who whirled about the room.

"So Rachel and I will go and collect him first thing and bring him straight back here," she went on as she worked. "Give him a chance to settle in and catch his breath." Observing my face, she added hastily, "Then perhaps you could come over tomorrow evening?"

I nodded. "I can think of nothing I would like better."

"He's coming home . . . Dan is coming home!" She pressed her hands together as children do when anticipation surges in them.

She smiled in slow wonderment, shaking her head, then she was off again, ferreting out a tablecloth from one set of drawers, some mismatched table mats from another. On an impulse, emboldened by her elation, I caught her about the waist as she spun past, pulling her to me, and she momentarily submitted, resting her cheek against my shoulder.

"He's fifteen now," I said softly in her ear. "Just bear that in mind, won't you? You must prepare yourself. It's going to be a tremendous shock."

She nodded, her lovely brown eyes blazing with this new light.

"*Fifteen!*" she repeated wonderingly. "Fifteen . . ."

"Nearly old enough to marry. To drive a car. Remember how thrown you were that time you bumped into Amman?"

At this her eyes widened with an incredulity that even as I watched clouded into melancholy.

"He'll have been through a great deal," I said.

She glanced down, her voice a whisper. "I know that. Don't you think I know that?"

Then she extracted herself from my arms, and I couldn't but reproach myself for so clumsily puncturing her girlish joie de vivre. For with the sadness came this familiar turning away.

"Just a few hours to wait now," I said, hoping to reinflate her mood. "Then Dan will be back—home again!"

She bit her lip, nodding as if to humor me, but her eyes slid away to the window, a troubled frown dulling their earlier brilliance.

"Where on earth can he have been all this time?" she asked, her hand flying to her mouth to stifle a sob.

I attempted to take her in my arms again, but she shrugged me off and I stood back feeling helpless, wondering what I might say to remedy matters.

It was Rachel's call from upstairs that broke the silence. She had finished the WELCOME HOME banner and needed someone to help her carry it down. I muttered something about how we must both count our blessings at this astonishing turn of events before leaving Annie lost in her thoughts.

14

As you will doubtless understand only too well, the following day proved interminable. I could only presume Annie's very silence was proof of Dan's safe arrival. If he hadn't been on the train she would surely have called. I visualized a great deal of hugging and weeping. A frank and tearful account on his part of all that had occurred. Much reciprocal hand-wringing on hers. Throughout the day I marked their imagined progress by my wristwatch. When lunchtime came, I thought of the three of them sitting down to their chicken Kiev and apple crumble. Annie had warned me that I shouldn't expect to hear from her before the evening, and though I had somehow whiled away the daylight hours, now it was dark, I returned to restively pace the flat. Several times when impatience got the better of me, I called her, only to be rebuffed by the voice mail. In desperation I switched the radio on then off, flicked through numerous television channels before turning to the day's paper, my eyes traveling sightlessly across the columns of print. I had just drained the last of the wine and was wondering whether I had time to nip down to the off-license for a new bottle when the phone finally rang.

I couldn't tell whether the emotion that choked Annie's voice was laughter or tears before it dawned on me that once again it was both.

"Well?"

"Oh my God. I can't tell you . . . just the most extraordinary day."

She struggled wordlessly for some moments. "I mean just *extraordinary*."

"So everything went—"

"Yes, yes. He's upstairs now! Fast asleep. Absolutely exhausted."

Once again there was a long silence while she wept. Though she made several attempts to resume, new waves of tears kept overcoming her. Eventually, she managed to continue: "I waited and waited at the station. We were there so early, you see. When the train came in, I went to stand by the barrier, and then suddenly—*suddenly*—there he was! He just appeared through the crowds. Can you imagine that! Can you imagine?"

She might easily have let him walk straight past if it hadn't been for the fact that he was the only unaccompanied teenager among the hundreds of disembarking passengers flooding through the gates. For he was both taller and leaner than when she had last seen him, and his fair hair was long now, falling into his eyes and over his collar. As he drew nearer, her eyes flew momentarily to his hand—and there, there was the little smudged D. Instantly, her heart had soared.

"Dan!"

He stopped uncertainly and nodded, his eyes wide with apprehension. He looked so alone and afraid that, quite overcome, she threw her arms about him, showering his face with kisses and weeping without restraint, while he stood, neither resisting nor yet submitting, but with a shy smile hovering at his lips and his eyes downcast. She kept pulling away to look at him in disbelief and wonder—"*Oh, let me look at you!*"—before seizing him rapturously in her arms again. He was without doubt a young man now. And handsome. There was no denying her boy was handsome. All about them was the sound of commuters hurrying by, a bustling purposeful hubbub, while here the two of them stood: the extraordinary revelation of him once again in her arms, the warmth of his breath against her cheek.

"You won't recognize him," she said now. "You'll be amazed. He must be almost as tall as you, now. Taller, perhaps." Her voice was filled with elation.

At last, reluctantly releasing him, Annie turned to see how Rachel shrank from them. Was he ready to meet his sister? she asked, and Dan nodded with the same apprehensive expression he had first cast upon her. She gestured for

Rachel to come forward, and the girl did so reluctantly, offering a timid handshake, after which the two of them stood so awkwardly tongue-tied that Annie couldn't resist putting her arms about them and drawing them together.

Where is his bag? she asked, as brother and sister sprang apart to stand once more surveying each other from afar. Annie was looking about for it, momentarily panic-stricken, and he had to remind her that he hadn't brought one, that he had nothing but the clothes he was wearing. It took a moment to absorb this fact before a wave of renewed foreboding passed through her and she had to force her mind from the multitude of questions that rose in a clamorous swarm.

"Well, we'll just have to take you shopping, won't we," she said with forced lightness. All the way across the concourse to the car park she kept turning to look at him, her heart leaping and soaring at the sight of her only son, her firstborn, once more restored to her. She longed to ask if he remembered her, for the blankness behind his eyes when he saw her had undeniably suggested otherwise, yet instinct told her she must give him some time now to gather himself.

Once in the car, still too dazed to properly concentrate, she almost immediately lost her bearings in the maze of diversions that had sprung up around King's Cross. Construction workers in fluorescent jackets swarmed everywhere, and a silence fell in the car as she snaked her head this way and that, trying to decipher the temporary road signs.

"Is Glasgow very far?" Rachel asked, to which Dan nodded. "And do *all* the men wear kilts?"

"Shhh," Annie scolded. "Remember what I told you. No questions. I think poor Dan must be completely shattered."

"Couldn't sleep," he affirmed after a silence that had stretched on uncomfortably. Annie reached forward to turn up the music on the radio, and he settled against the seat, tipping his head back and closing his eyes, as if to end all further communication. He did look extremely pale, Annie thought, glancing anxiously between his face and the road. But moments later when she looked, she found he had opened his eyes again.

At this, Rachel couldn't resist making another attempt to engage him. "Chip's waiting for you at home! We've been looking after him," she told him eagerly. "And everything in your room is exactly how it was when you left."

On their way, Annie had warned her that Dan appeared to be suffering from some kind of memory loss and that she was not to be disconcerted if he appeared confused. Noting his silence, Rachel added helpfully, "Chip's your pet gecko." But Dan's eyes remained fixed upon the passing city. "You do remember him, don't you?" she persisted doggedly.

"No," he said in a hollow voice. A long pause. He turned to address them both. "I don't remember nothing."

At the front door of the house, both Annie and Rachel hung back to allow Dan to be the first to step ceremonially across the threshold. She could tell from his pallor that he was in shock. Indeed, they all were.

When the three of them sat down to eat breakfast, Annie found herself unable to tear her eyes from him, nodding and beaming absurdly at his every gesture. As they ate, Rachel and Annie attempted a little nervous small talk, but Dan kept his eyes on his plate, only now and then throwing quick darting glances about the room.

"Does it all seem strangely familiar?" Annie couldn't resist asking anxiously, but he shook his head and lowered his eyes to his plate again.

When they had finished, Annie began to clear the plates, and at once Rachel jumped up from the table.

"Can I show Dan his room?"

"Of course." Annie smiled. "But then you must come straight down again and let Dan have a little time to himself."

He rose and followed Rachel into the hall, looking about him more boldly now. Annie had stood listening to the sound of the stairs creak as they made their ascent and Rachel's animated chatter.

"He just needs a moment to catch his breath," she explained in an attempt to quell Rachel's disappointment when she reluctantly presented herself to her mother again. But it wasn't long before Annie herself hastened upstairs to check on him, overcome by a sudden terror that he might have vanished as mysteriously as he had appeared. She found him standing in front of his shelves, touching his old possessions in turn, taking the weight of each one in his hands. It was almost, she said, as if he was savoring the scent of something deeply embedded and much missed. As she watched, still unaware that he was being observed, he had walked over to the bed and run a hand along his old bedspread before letting out a low, wondering whistle.

"Are you . . . Is everything . . ." she ventured, and he started so violently at the sound of her voice, spinning round with an expression so heartrending, she automatically stepped forward to put her arms about him. Yet he had made the tiniest hand gesture, as if to forestall her, and she backed away again, filling the strained silence with a stammering platitude about putting the kettle on, before retreating downstairs.

I sat taking all of this in for a moment. "It will take time," I said after a long pause, realizing that Annie was crying again. "Things are bound to feel very awkward and strange at first."

"It will take time," she echoed.

I asked how severe she thought his amnesia was, and she fell silent for a moment, reflecting. It was very hard to know. He had said so little. When she went to say good night, she told him that as soon as he felt ready, they would sit down and talk. She wasn't going to rush him, but there was a great deal she was going to need to ask. He had nodded, appearing so defenseless as he lay beneath the covers that once again she longed to offer some gesture of affection. Yet she was conscious that every time she moved towards him, he gave the impression of shrinking from her. So she compromised with a businesslike kiss on his forehead before tucking him in.

"Is there anything I can get you?" she whispered, but he only shook his head, and settled into the pillows, appearing touchingly childlike again. "This," she said, reaching out to brush his hair from his eyes, "is the most wonderful thing that has ever happened to me. To have found you again. To see for myself that you are safe and well after all." Once again he nodded meekly, and she switched out the light. "If you want anything, if you wake in the night and are frightened, please just come and find me."

Ten minutes later she put her head round the door again to find he had fallen into a deep sleep, and unable to resist the opportunity to study him further, she stood for some while watching his shadowed face and listening to the rise and fall of his breath. It was only the thought of how anxious I would be to hear from her that eventually compelled her to tear herself away.

"I'll be there as quickly as I can," I cried, leaping to my feet, unable to wait a moment longer. "If I can just quietly put my head round his door, it might all start to feel a little more real."

At this there was an uncomfortable silence.

"I've been thinking very carefully about this, Julian. And I've come to a rather tricky decision—one I hope you'll understand. You see, he's obviously in a very fragile state, and I honestly don't think he could handle meeting anyone else just yet. Luke Holland told me to expect a period of adjustment and recovery, and I'm only just beginning to understand what he meant."

"I see."

"So I've decided we will have no visitors. No police and all that circus that will follow in their wake—all those journalists and photographers back on our doorstep again. At least for the first few days, anyway. Can you imagine how terrifying it would be for him to have to run the gauntlet of that baying mob? The more relaxed and stress-free the next few days are, the better his chances of making a full recovery are going to be."

"What kind of time frame do you have in mind?"

"Well, I don't know. I hadn't really . . . At least a fortnight, I suppose."

"A fortnight! Annie! Surely I could just shoot over this evening and—"

"No. I'm afraid it really wouldn't be fair on him. He needs total rest now and complete privacy. What if he suddenly woke up and found you standing there, goggling at him? He'd be frightened out of his wits."

A horrible suspicion stole upon me.

"If this is because you still hold me in some way accountable, I really think—"

"This isn't about you, Julian. It's about what's best for Dan," she said, with such severity I saw there was nothing to be done but concede.

"Of course, of course," I backtracked, hastily trying to quell my disappointment. "Dan's welfare is paramount. I'll be standing by until you give me the word. But if you need anything, Annie, anything at all, please don't hesitate to call me, will you? I'll be waiting in the wings. I want you to remember that."

13

Annie took me at my word and, as that first week unfolded, would call each day to report on their progress. I won't deny that despite my impatience I took some comfort in my new role of confidant after our weeks of estrangement, and soon found myself looking forward to her call each evening, once she had given the children supper and persuaded them to retire to their bedrooms. I would make a little ceremony of it, settling into the battered armchair with a glass of wine poured in readiness.

On the second day, she told me that Dan remained guarded, speaking only when directly addressed. She had to caution herself not to fuss over him, to give him space. His old surliness had vanished without a trace. Instead, on the rare occasions when he spoke, there was now a disconcerting formality. She found it almost impossible to tear her eyes from him whenever they were together. Nor could she resist attempting to coax a phrase or two if an opportunity presented itself, while the things that once vexed her—the picking up of damp towels, the preparation and clearing away of meals—now struck her as gratifying labors of love.

Her rapture at the handsome young man who had returned was clouded only by a lingering wistfulness for the little boy who had slipped away—together with a dread at what he might have undergone in the lost years. For from her tentative inquiries thus far it was apparent that his memory loss was indeed profound. Though she claimed to be optimistic that he would in time resume the threads of his old life, the uncertainty in her voice told a different story.

On the third day I was pleased to hear her sounding rather more buoyant. Once again Dan had slept until lunchtime. He was obviously completely shattered. But eventually he had risen and wolfed down a vast quantity of the shepherd's pie she had spent the morning preparing. Then they had walked to the river together, where Dan exclaimed in astonishment at the great sweep of water.

"What is that?" he asked.

"The river Thames," she answered. "Surely you must remember the river!"

But he had only shaken his head, watching the scullers pass to and fro with fascination. There had apparently been a series of such firsts. It was as if his mind had emptied itself—rather as a damaged hard drive might, she said musingly. She seemed to find this analogy obscurely helpful, returning to it several times in the ensuing days, always in the same intent tone, as if through dint of repetition it might yield some deeper insight.

On the fourth day she told me that she often found herself transported back to the time she spent in hospital with Dan after he was born three weeks prematurely. On the verge of closure, the hospital had been allowed to fall into a dismal state of disrepair, yet as she lay in the deserted ward with Dan asleep beside her in a Perspex bassinet and sunlight slanting in through the grimy windows, she had experienced a sense of purpose she had never known before. The clamor of the world had receded, her sole objective to nurture new life. Now, with the two of them closeted together in the house all day, it struck her that they had in some odd way come full circle.

To my dismay, something about this tender description stirred an unwelcome echo of the strange dreams that had so tormented me in the weeks after our separation. Indeed, as that week unfolded, I found her accounts of their time together created a sensation of voyeurism that was discomforting and compelling in almost equal measure.

On the fifth day, I had to travel to Madrid on business, but the distance was overridden by the continuing candor of Annie's confidences. I had checked into the Hotel Preciados and was only just unpacking my things when the phone rang and there was Annie again, whispering—for fear Dan might overhear—so intimately into my ear that at once I was a priest receiving confession.

"This morning I crept into his room while he was sleeping. I couldn't resist it. He had his hands crossed on his chest. And his hair . . . his hair was flowing over the pillow, like a halo round his head. I stood there for ages just watching him. He looked so peaceful, so amazingly beautiful as he lay there, he could have been sculpted out of marble."

There was something so idealized about this account that for the first time a new and rather startling misgiving came to me. Surely, after all those years of longing, she wouldn't have simply resorted to inventing him? Could such a thing be possible? Utterly outlandish though it seemed, it would nonetheless explain why I was being held at arm's length in this way.

So it was something of a relief when she so readily agreed in a rather more pragmatic tone to my suggestion that the time had come to try to establish exactly what he could and couldn't remember. Yet when I called her later that day, anxious to hear what had emerged, she confessed with an apologetic laugh that her nerve had completely failed her.

"He's still so fragile, Julian. I'm terrified I might say the wrong thing and end up making everything worse." She appeared to weigh something for a moment. "And I suppose, if I'm completely honest, I'm just not quite ready to face some of the things he might tell me. I know that sounds terrible . . ."

I thought of our searches through Bayswater and King's Cross and could only presume she was alluding to the distressing fate of the children we had glimpsed there. "Well, if you really don't feel up to the task, Annie, then we must leave it in the hands of the police, since they will have specialist counselors who can handle the matter with the necessary sensitivity."

This suggestion was evidently the impetus she required, for the very next day, while Rachel was at school, Annie reported that she had finally tackled the issue with Dan over lunch. As she set the dishes down, she asked very casually how he was feeling now that he had been home for a week, to which he shrugged, chewing his food and frowning as if giving the question careful consideration.

"Confused," he said at length.

"That social worker—Luke Holland—told me that when you turned up at the refuge, you couldn't remember your name or how old you were."

He nodded.

"And now?"

Another shrug. Another shake of the head. "Nothing."

"So you can't offer any explanation for how you came to be in Scotland?" she persisted.

"No. I only remember that bloke asking if he could help. I remember feeling scared. Then they found your number in my pocket."

"Do you have any idea how long you've been gone?"

He shook his head.

"What would you say if I told you it had been three years?"

"Three years?" he repeated in astonishment. "*Three years!*"

So he hadn't seen any of the appeals? Hadn't had any idea that she was looking for him? No. He didn't know what she was talking about, he replied, sounding panic-stricken.

She told him about the death of his father and her plans to remarry. She described her growing despair as the police search failed to throw any light on what had become of him. She told him she had pinned posters about the district and contacted every homeless organization she could think of. That despite all evidence to the contrary, she had always remained resolute that somewhere he was alive and well.

After hearing this, Dan had sat in silence for some time, appearing deeply moved, and Annie felt it best to leave the conversation there—at least for the time being. It was too much to digest at one sitting, she could see that. These events that had spanned a number of years, compressed into just a few minutes.

She had relayed all this with a sense of urgency. Now at last she paused and sighed.

"So I told him that in a few days, we would talk again."

"In a few days?" I echoed in dismay. "But what about the police? Shouldn't you at the very least be contacting Angela Kofi now?"

"I did mention the possibility to Dan. But as he pointed out, the Glasgow police will have set the wheels in motion. Every time the phone rings, I expect it to be them. Though to be perfectly honest, the longer they take, the better for Dan, as far as I'm concerned."

After I put the phone down, I sat for a long while reflecting deeply on all that she had described.

The next day, Annie took Dan to the doctor. She told him what little she knew of her son's story, though she implied that three years had been no more than a matter of weeks. Since his return, she said, he appeared to be suffering from a profound memory loss and she was concerned that he might have sustained a head injury of some kind. The doctor examined him carefully, before pronouncing him "as fit as a fiddle." He said that the amnesia was as likely to be psychological as physical in origin, in which case it would be a matter for specialist investigation. He advised her to give Dan another week to settle in, and if there was no sign of improvement in that time, he would refer him for an assessment.

That evening, after the children had gone to bed, Annie Googled *Amnesia* and came across something called *Dissociative Fugue*. It was a form of amnesia, she explained to me later, in which someone undergoing an intense emotional conflict impulsively leaves home.

"Sometimes they end up miles away. No idea who they are, or where it is they have come from. They often just start a completely new life wherever it is they happen to have ended up. Apparently it's a condition that can be triggered by some kind of subconscious longing to escape whatever it is that caused the conflict in the first place."

There was a pause while she considered this. "For the first time I feel as if the pieces of the jigsaw might be starting to slot into place."

Despite the fact that autumn was well advanced, the weather had remained unseasonably fine, each day bringing a blue sky more luminous than the last. Now gusts of wind began to wrench the only remaining leaves from the trees, sending great rustling sighs among the branches, and as that first week drew to a close, Annie reported happily that there were some modest signs of progress. Dan had spent that morning poring over the framed collage of photographs with Rachel, who had seized the opportunity to regale him rather self-importantly with the family history they recorded, gratified to find in him such an unexpectedly attentive listener. Later the children went through Dan's cupboards, taking out old toys that had been stored there over the years. Of course they had both long ago outgrown the things they found, but their nostalgia touched her. It was a reminder, she said, that he was in many ways still just a small boy at heart.

Eventually, they settled upon a box of Legos and lay for some while creating an elaborate cityscape that stretched in every direction across the bedroom floor. It wasn't long, however, before a dispute broke out, and Rachel fled to her room in tears.

Annie sounded surprisingly cheerful about this turn of events. "I can't tell you how lovely it is to hear the sound of normal family life resuming," she said with a laugh.

Though I don't think she intended it, her comment took so little account of my absence I couldn't help but be pierced through the heart by it.

12

At long last, the invitation came. And when it did, it was typically last-minute and offhand. *Going to fireworks in Fishers Meadows tonight,* Annie's text message ran. *Why not join us?*

Though the sky was only just darkening, there was already a faint crackling of distant fireworks as I settled myself into the back of the cab, beset by a potent combination of apprehension and curiosity. I suppose, though I didn't think of it then, the far-off festivities served to heighten the impression that this was in some way a momentous journey. That whatever lay at its end would be life-changing.

My Serbian driver was in a gregarious mood, and I let him talk while I watched the trails of brilliant light that burst every now and then high above the rooftops in the distance as we traveled. I felt rather as a penitent must who comes in a state of great trepidation and humility to seek forgiveness.

* * *

By the time I arrived at the close it was completely dark, and a narrow gap in the half-drawn curtains tantalizingly suggested something of the homely warmth within. I had hurried all the way, but now I stood for some moments on the doorstep, attempting to compose myself before summoning the courage to ring the bell.

Annie looked pale when she opened the door, instantly placing a finger to her lips as if to indicate that I must ask no questions, before gesturing for me to go ahead of her into the sitting room. Yet overcome by an inexplicable failure of nerve, I hung back and after a moment's hesitation, Annie, tsking impatiently, stepped in front of me and pushed the door open.

"Dan?" She spoke his name in an undertone, and he turned, rising at once to his feet. How tall and slender he was, the residual bloom of childhood combining with a striking athletic manliness! Just as Annie had said, it was a remarkable metamorphosis. The twitchy alertness with which he appraised me reminded me of a racing animal, his quick shrewd eyes never leaving my face, as if anxious to discern my response. How long his fair hair, now falling into his eyes! How broad his shoulders! I saw that though I had warned Annie to prepare herself, I had made no such preparations myself. Even as I reached out to take his hand, I found that all powers of speech eluded me. With a great effort of will I managed to inquire in a croaking voice how he was, to which he replied that he supposed he was doing all right.

"We're just taking it one day at a time, aren't we, Danny?"

Annie interjected, her head pivoting between us as the silence lengthened. She tried to laugh. "I think Julian's in shock at how much you've changed." She glanced fearfully at him. "And Dan—you look as if you're wondering who on earth this strange man can be. Surely you remember Julian, don't you? Now that he's here?"

"I told you," he said.

"I know, but I hoped when you saw him, you might . . ." She turned to me with a desperate smile. "You see? Everything—still *just a blank*."

It was a moment or two before I remembered his hand clasped in mine, at once releasing it, stepping back, and gesturing instead to the heavens.

"This has to be one of the . . ." I began, turning to Annie. "I mean, talk about . . ." I tried again, addressing Rachel instead. Then, turning finally to appeal to Dan himself: "Whatever became of that little boy then?" I knew perfectly well it was lame even as I offered it, though absurdly he glanced downwards, as if the last vestiges of childhood might still be seen slipping away.

"I honestly think I would have walked past you in the street without a second glance," I said. Then I looked at him, and he looked at me—and once again an awkward silence fell on the room. I had come determined to befriend him, to put behind us any lingering reserve. Why, then, was I troubled by something lurking just out of sight, at the edge of my thoughts? All these years later, I can think of no other way to describe it. I glanced down at his hand and found the little tattoo, just as Annie had done. There it was. The familiar smudged blue D.

I cleared my throat. "Well, welcome." *Oh, that was it, that was more like it.* "Welcome home, Dan."

Then before I could say anything more, Annie was stepping forward again with a smile of radiant relief, clapping her hands and ushering us all into the hall. "Okay. Coats. Scarves. Gloves. Come on, guys. We need to get going."

At the park we made slow progress through the crush of people. Close to the bonfire, faces shone in the flickering amber light, while beyond them the crowds gathered from every direction. I walked a step or two ahead, trying to clear a passage as best I could while Annie and the children followed slowly behind. After Dan's disappearance she had avoided crowds whenever possible, fearful of how easily Rachel might be lost. She was gripping their hands in hers, and though Dan appeared to be submitting to this indignity without protest, he kept his head bowed.

"The first time you came here," she spoke in a self-consciously chatty voice, as if to calm herself, "you couldn't have been much more than five, and it was a complete disaster. You were so terrified by all the noise and people that you wept and wept, and Daddy and I had to take you straight home again. It was years—literally *years*—before I could persuade you to come again!" She smiled up at him. "You were never a great one for bangs and whistles. Looking back, I can see that you were always a rather sensitive child."

At that moment, a great trunk of wood leaped into flame, with an explosion like a gun going off, and as the fire flew higher, new faces loomed from the darkness. It was then that one of them, a stout woman in her fifties, turned and caught sight of us. I saw her totter back, before uttering a squawk of amazement.

"It isn't, is it? It can't be! Oh my God, it is! It's Dan!"

At once she came forward with her arms outstretched to seize him in an embrace so all-encompassing he appeared to vanish inside the voluminous folds of her coat while she rocked him to and fro.

"How you've grown! Dearie me, how you've grown . . ."

Then she held Dan at arm's length, pinching his cheeks with such savage gusto I thought he would surely protest, yet he endured it stoically.

"Barbara used to babysit you," Annie murmured like a diligent undersecretary in his ear. Dan nodded guardedly, shuffling backwards once Barbara had released her grip, as if to safety.

"I always knew you'd be back! Didn't I keep saying that, Annie? Dearie me! Your mum's been to hell and back, I can tell you. To hell and back."

Then the woman called to her husband, who turned towards us, starting at the sight of Dan and calling out as he hastened forward in a tone midway between belligerence and humor, "Where the bloody hell have you been all these years?"

I stepped forward and caught him by the arm.

"Please—try to keep your voice down, would you," I whispered urgently.

He raised his hands, sheepishly muttering that he was only joking, that he meant nothing by it, before reaching out to clap Dan on the shoulder.

"Rachel told the kids you was back," he said in a reverent tone. "We thought she must be having a laugh, didn't we, Barbs? Christ Almighty! It's a bloody miracle, isn't it. Isn't it?" he said again, turning to nudge me in the ribs.

"Yes, yes. A miracle."

His wife pulled Dan to her again, kissing him on each cheek before finally releasing him, her hand fluttering first to her over-brimming eyes, and then to her heart, apologizing all the while for her emotion. The flames had died away again, and with the ebbing of the light Dan's face was lost once more in darkness, though the stoop of his shoulders suggested an intense mortification.

"Keep him close, keep him close," Barbara said, gripping Annie's arm before turning away, noisily trumpeting into a handkerchief.

To my alarm, two more families now emerged from among the crowds, eagerly waiting to pay their respects: a family of four who Annie explained to Dan lived a few houses down; then a boy who turned out to be Amman Kazi, accompanied by his mother, who stepped forward to gawp at Dan with undisguised fascination as Annie whispered an explanation in his ear again.

"I saw your mum, then I saw that lady crying and hugging

you," Amman said, "and I was like, no way, man—that must be Dan!"

Dan shook the hand he offered without enthusiasm. "Where've you been hiding yourself then?" Amman asked, and this time it was Annie who stepped forward.

"I'm terribly sorry, Amman, but I'm afraid Dan really isn't up to answering any questions just yet."

He shrugged. "Can I just take a quick picture?"

Annie glanced towards Dan, who nodded, and the two of them stood side by side while Amman's mother held up her mobile phone, the flash momentarily highlighting their stiff smiles. Now the family of four came forward to take their leave of him, offering a quick dip of the head, or a comradely pat on the arm, and he nodded graciously to each of them in turn. Then with a high whistling shriek and a tremendous crackling the firework display started up, and the four of us turned our faces to the starbursts of light that shimmered in the skies above our heads, while murmurs of pleasure rose in waves on every side.

11

First thing the next morning, I hastened back to Fishers Meadows. Right up until the moment Annie opened the door with that disarming smile, I was determined to have it out with her. "Something is amiss," I was going to say. "Something about this whole business doesn't smell quite right."

Even as I took the seat she proffered, noting how she sashayed about the kitchen, humming softly beneath her breath to the music that filled the room, even then I was still puzzling how best to phrase it. There were fresh flowers in a jug on the table. Could it really be three years since she had last bought flowers for the house? And the smell of warm yeast filled the air. I had entirely forgotten her bread-making skills—how many of her enthusiasms had lain dormant for all those years?

From the moment I woke after a restless night, my resolve had been absolute. Yet everything about her now expressed such a joyful resumption that I couldn't help but survey her delight. I had forgotten too how much she once loved music. How sweet her voice as she sang along. And somehow my resolve was dissipating among this festive blaze of flowers and homely scents of baking. Certainly the words I uttered were not at all what I had expected to hear myself say.

"I owe you a sincere apology, Annie. Evidently, miracles do occur, after all."

She was nodding, her face alight with wonder. "I have to keep pinching myself."

"A second chance."

"Exactly! Exactly that—a second chance."

"I shall make every effort now to befriend Dan. I just want you to know that."

She was watching me intently. "Thank you."

"Can we let bygones be bygones?"

She nodded quickly, her eyes filling with tears, before taking up a cloth and beginning to briskly wipe the table down. Very soon, she began to hum again, lightly skimming my hair with her fingertips as she passed my chair—rather as one might contentedly caress a pet—and there was something so beguiling in her distracted affection that for the life of me, I could no longer recall the pressing nature of my unease.

When I put my head round the sitting room door to check on Dan, he was gripping the controls of a computer game, so absorbed in defending himself against the assassin whose blazing guns lit up the screen, he barely appeared to note my presence. I watched him for some moments, taking him in all over again, marveling at the sight of him reclining there in his pajamas. A latter-day miracle indeed. Returning to the kitchen, I found a steaming cup of coffee awaiting me.

"That was something of a hero's welcome last night, wasn't it?" I said.

Annie nodded, a rapturous expression passing over her face at the recollection. "First thing this morning, there's Barbara on the doorstep with a cake she's baked for Dan. Obviously angling to be invited in. So I had to explain that we were just taking things slowly, one step at a time, I said. Of course, she was all agog to know where he'd been—why he'd stayed away so long. I told her we just didn't know yet. I explained that Rachel had been wrong to say anything and begged her not to mention it to anyone quite yet. She promised that they wouldn't breathe a word. She only wanted what was best for Dan, she said. And then she got all weepy again."

Annie bent to take the bread out of the oven, lifting it between gloved hands and sliding it onto a wire rack to cool. I wondered hopefully if she might be about to extend an invitation to join them for lunch.

"What does Dan actually do with himself all day?" I asked, settling myself in my old spot at the table.

"Well, I try to leave him to his own devices as much as I can, and usually he doesn't get up much before lunch. Then he'll just watch TV or play computer games. Of course, I'd never have allowed such a thing in the old days, would I? But I think it's what he needs now. And little by little he's definitely becoming less . . . watchful. Though it's true he still doesn't say much."

She had begun to chop onions, before pausing with the knife in midair. "But then I suppose he's never really been the greatest of communicators, has he?" A sadness clouded her face until a new thought struck her, and she rallied again.

"Earlier in the week, Emma brought over some old family movies. Honestly, you should have seen me. I got terribly emotional."

"And Dan?"

"Oh, he was completely engrossed. Particularly by the stuff when he was little. There was one bit, where he's playing cricket in the garden with David. He couldn't have been much more than four, and he's struggling to hold a bat almost as tall as he is. He asked to see it three or four times. I thought perhaps it was bringing back some memories, but he said no, he just liked to see what a good laugh he used to have with his dad."

Afterwards, she went on, he had appeared noticeably more forthcoming, even agreeing to accompany Annie on a shopping trip to replenish his lost wardrobe, and wherever the two of them went she found herself buying him little gifts. Trinkets. Gadgets. In fact, the truth was, she laughed, she found it impossible to refuse him anything and had spoiled him horribly.

Annie slid the onions into the frying pan, their familiar pungency sending up a comforting aroma.

"And what now?" I asked.

"How d'you mean?"

"Well, there's quite a list of things to be tackled, isn't there? Where in heaven's name are you planning to start?"

"I'm not sure I follow you, Julian."

"First and foremost there's the police. Obviously. Since they haven't yet called, I presume you must contact them. And then there's Dan's schooling. Not to mention, on the basis of what your GP told you, the possibility of a consultation with a neurologist."

She was listening with a faintly mocking smile.

"How did we ever cope without you?" she laughed.

"Well?"

"To be perfectly honest, I'm not really planning to *do* anything. I've already told you. The police will call any day now."

"But there are proper procedures that need to be implemented now—questions that will simply have to—"

"Oh, Julian. Please!" Annie set the chopping board before me, together with a knife and a bag of mushrooms. "You're forever trying to schedule everything. Why not, just for once, live dangerously and try going with the flow? My sister thinks it's absolutely hilarious I ever went out with someone so completely anal about everything."

I was about to resume my lobbying when I found myself momentarily distracted by the odd faraway smile that had crept across her face. She coiled a strand of hair about her finger, before fixing me with a disconcertingly mischievous expression.

"She asked after you, by the way."

"Who did?"

"Emma."

Something in her arch tone managed to convey that the inquiry might not have been an entirely favorable one.

"She wanted to know if there was any chance that you and I might be planning to complete the fairy-tale ending by getting back together again."

"Did she indeed?" I answered, taking off my glasses in some haste and beginning to polish them assiduously. It seemed to take an eternity for her to continue. "So what did you say?" I prompted at last, replacing the glasses and finding her face still lit by the same puzzling smile.

"I said that if all of this has taught me anything—it's that you should never say never."

A little aria rose absurdly within me. How greedily I squirreled the phrase away, intending to examine it again the moment I was alone. Now it was Annie's turn to feign absorption as she vigorously stirred the frying pan, though the ghost of that odd smile still hovered about her lips. I very much doubted whether Annie's sister would have responded to the possibility of any reconciliation between us with much enthusiasm, for my relationship with Emma had remained as constrained as the day Annie—with a certain defiant pride—first introduced us. It was a meeting it still pained me to recall.

* * *

On the way there Annie had explained that in her mid-thirties, having dated men all her adult life, her sister had fallen head over heels in love with another woman. Though their family were initially taken aback, the relationship had proved a very happy one. Emma and Jane now had a son, Zak, who, though Emma was the biological mother, called them respectively Mum and Mummy. Listening to all this with some surprise, I did my best to appear unfazed. Our courtship was still in its infancy, and I hadn't as yet succumbed to the role of old fogy she had begun to teasingly ascribe to me.

Their home when we got there proved perfectly pleasant: a more style-conscious and ordered household than Annie's, and Jane a smilingly affable presence. Aware that I had entered a politically correct minefield without the necessary qualifications, I resolved to proceed with due caution, and probably it was this that undid me. For despite my best efforts, the conversation remained so stilted, I suspect it was a relief to us all when the time came to leave. As Emma and her baby waited at the door to say good-bye, I paused to chuck him under the chin.

"Were you shocked when Annie told you we had a gaybe?" she asked, surveying her offspring with pride.

"I beg your pardon?"

This provoked a burst of laughter from all three.

"A baby born to a gay couple—the kind of setup that gets the *Mail* so hot under the collar."

A deft response might have saved me. Unfortunately, none was forthcoming.

"As a matter of fact, I'm rather impressed by your domestic arrangements," I countered. "I think you're both tremendously brave."

"How kind of you to say so," she said with a gracious dip of the head.

Annie and I had driven home in a silence freighted with tension.

"What on earth possessed you to use the word *brave*?" she said at last, burying her face in her hands. "Jesus, Julian. You made it sound as if they were heroically enduring some terrible misfortune."

It was another of those moments in which we felt the fault line widen a fraction further between us. In every encounter since, Emma and I had eyed each other with cordial unease.

I was just wondering how best to pursue Annie's tantalizing allusion to a reconciliation when the door flew open and Rachel came running in. She threw her arms about my neck, eagerly reminding me of my promise to take her out for an hour. So with Annie's permission we set off across the meadows, and she skipped and danced before me like a little sprite released from captivity. The great domed sky above us was flecked by the feathery brushstrokes of cirrus castellanus. For the first time I noticed that the trees were now bare and the landscape once more clothed in Rembrandt's colors. The cold air brought a rush of exhilaration. So this was the kind of world we lived in! I looked about me, beaming. When all seemed hopeless, a lost child might be found. And an estranged relationship unexpectedly revive. What remarkable dividends a little patience and understanding could reap!

We paused to pluck the blackberries still to be found among the brambles that grew in dense clumps in the hedgerows. Presently we came to the towpath and stopped to watch as a long rowing boat filled with giggling schoolgirls came abreast of us on the river.

"SOS! SOS!" they were screeching as their boat spun around before gently striking the bank and shearing off again, at which half their number doubled up over their oars, laughing so helplessly they were entirely deaf to their cox's angry remonstrations as he shouted through his megaphone.

Though we walked on in silence, their wild hilarity still hung on the air, its mood informing my tone when I spoke.

"So, what a fortnight you have had! How has it been?"

Rachel looked down at her feet, a troubled crease between her eyes. "Fine."

"Fine?" I gently teased, but she only offered a little shrug of her shoulders, her expression impenetrable.

"I imagine it must be quite extraordinary. A long-lost brother just appearing again like that after all these years."

"Yes," she said, speaking with a careful primness. "Mum keeps saying how lucky we are. She's like a completely different person—smiling and singing all day."

"Well, you heard Barbara's husband last night. It was a miracle, he said. And he's right. A very remarkable thing has occurred. It will take a little time for everything to settle down again."

She nodded doubtfully.

"And what do you make of this brother of yours now he's back?"

"He's . . ." She frowned as she walked. "He's quite nice, I suppose."

I laughed again. I had never known her so unforthcoming.

"And yet a stranger?"

She glanced quickly at me, nodding several times.

"Mum says we must do everything we can to make him feel welcome." She had echoed Annie's earnest tone exactly.

"Well, she's right. I think we must."

"She took him shopping on Wednesday and bought him tons of presents and stuff."

"Did she, indeed?" I smiled. "Well, perhaps it will cheer you up if I let you in on a little secret." I winked at her, pleased that I could recompense her with my news. "I don't want to get your hopes up too much, but it may be that Dan isn't the only one to be coming home again."

At this she only curled her lip and slashed disconsolately at the long grass with the flat of her hand. How mercurial children were! Yet nothing would dent my mood today.

"Now, why don't you and I see if we can spot any of the phantom horseman's tracks on the way home?"

She responded by tossing her hair with a loftiness that made her appear momentarily much older than her years. I had been about to take her hand but, thinking better of it, fell instead to humming a little Schubert, and we completed our walk without any further exchange.

Afterwards, once I had returned to my flat, I put a ready-made meal in the microwave and took stock. *Never say never*, Annie had said. Yet somehow, without her flirtatious delivery, the phrase no longer shone with the same promise. I had allowed myself to be diverted, I thought, watching the synthetic flicker of the flames. Left to her own devices, Annie would be only too capable of dithering for weeks. The sooner all these loose ends were tied up, the sooner our chances of reconciliation. I took it as a good omen that her reply to my text was so prompt.

A drink by the river—how lovely!

Any chance it might be just the two of us?

A moment later: *Will ask Dan if he can babysit.*

I waited the week out impatiently. We had agreed on a favorite pub we used to frequent in the old days, and I got there early enough to secure a window seat where we would be able to look out on the glitter of lights across the river.

At last I spotted her, hurrying along the darkened tow-path. Beside her trotted Rachel, and a little way behind, Dan. They came in a rush through the door, rosy-cheeked from the cold night air and sat down opposite me in a row, one after the other.

"It's still too early to leave him on his own," Annie offered in an apologetic whisper as they settled themselves, unwinding the long scarf from about her neck. "And now he's in a right old strop about having to come." She rolled her eyes.

At the very least, I thought, attempting to digest my disappointment as I queued to buy drinks, I might use this as an opportunity to ingratiate myself with Dan. But my heart wasn't really in it. As I set down the drinks before them, I asked him how he was getting on, and he muttered that he was feeling a bit tired.

"*She* woke me up too early," he said in a sullen tone.

"Actually it was nearly lunchtime," Annie responded, with mild indignation. "And the only reason I woke you was because yesterday you slept right through until tea."

At this he slumped back in his chair and folded his arms, restively jiggling one leg, and all attempts at further conversation faltered. A question about the World Cup was met with a shrug of indifference, and when I took out the bright new conkers I had picked up on my way, it was only Rachel whose eyes lit up. But she had no sooner snaked out a hand to seize one than she had registered Dan's stony indifference and promptly withdrawn it again.

A renewed silence fell upon all four of us. The children sipped their drinks, looking vacantly about the room, while Annie appeared distracted by the conversation at a neighboring table. Any moment now, I thought, they will be rising again to their feet, thanking me for the drinks, and buttoning themselves up against the cold. I reached over and touched Annie's hand.

"*Tu lui as parlé encore une fois?*"

Startled, she shook her head, looking quickly at Dan, though he appeared to be immersed in some little gadget he had taken from his pocket.

"*Mais tu as certainement téléphoné à la police?*"

Once again a sharp glance at Dan, followed by a negative shake.

"*Alors, qu'est-ce qui est arrivé à propos de l'école?*"

She folded her arms and pursed her lips, as if to make it clear she would not be drawn any further. Then, yawning widely, Dan set his game aside and rose to his feet, apparently to investigate the sounds of a boisterous game of pool being played at the far end of the bar, followed moments later by Rachel. There was no mistaking the look of panic that crossed Annie's face as she watched them go, her mouth opening as if to summon them back, before she slowly closed it again.

"Please, Julian," she muttered. "Can't we just enjoy a nice quiet drink? I'm really not in the mood for one of your lectures." She had fixed her attention on her hands now and was twisting her rings first one way, then the other.

"Can we at least agree that we must urgently find a school for him?"

Over the years I had become something of a connoisseur in reading her face, particularly the tensions expressed in the underlying muscles about her mouth, and I knew only too well that this pinched contraction didn't bode well.

"The trouble is, Julian, it would be putting the cart before the horse. You see, the school will only want to know where Dan has been all this while. And until I can answer that question, it frankly seems a bit premature."

An exasperated laugh broke from me.

"Which brings us back to where we began!" I exclaimed with barely disguised impatience. "Certain basic questions simply have to be addressed now. You must sit him down and ask him directly. Where has he been all this while? And how is it he has fed and clothed himself?"

"I keep telling you. I fully intend to. When the time is right."

"But it just strikes me it's one excuse after another, that's all. And meanwhile he's living in a kind of limbo."

She shifted resentfully, a shutter falling behind her eyes, and lifted her glass to drain her drink.

"For pity's sake, Annie, is the poor boy to live the rest of his life as a recluse? Surely the sooner it is all out in the open—the sooner we face whatever must be faced—the better it will be, for all of us." I leaned towards her. "What is it you are hoping to achieve by dragging your feet like this?"

Her mouth sagged; I saw the swift glassy glint of tears again. For the first time I noted the dark half-moons that cupped each eye.

"Look—I messed up, didn't I? And now I've been given a second chance, I'm *not* about to screw it up again. If you really think that so unreasonable, then frankly . . . frankly you can go to hell." She rose to her feet, bumping the table in her haste and calling impatiently for the children to join her. "All I ask—all I have ever asked—is that you let me handle this at my own pace, in my own way." She bent to collect their coats left draped across a chair, momentarily stumbling on a trailing arm. As if in response, a gale of laughter rose up from the neighboring table, and calling sharply to the children again, she retrieved first one coat, then the other as they tumbled to the floor, before bidding me a crisp good night.

"Good night. See you soon," I called after the children, but the three of them had hurried out into the darkness without so much as a backward glance.

10

In the days that followed, even the most banal things appeared charged with secret meaning. It was the season of the lost glove. Wherever I went, I glimpsed them lying discarded, and once one impaled on a gatepost, its fingers splayed imploringly to the skies, like some emblem of the falling world. Though I longed to lose myself in work, I found myself distracted by a regret that only deepened. How rashly I had forfeited the role of confidant so fleetingly bestowed upon me. My phone calls remained unanswered. Two text messages composed with a lighthearted humor it had taken some while to construct failed to raise a response of any kind.

I often wondered what could have possessed me to take a lease on a flat of such exceptional wretchedness. My windows looked out onto the dustbins at the back of the building, and the entire place smelled of brackish despair. I had wanted, I supposed, to make a statement of intent that this was to be no more than a pit stop, a temporary resting-place. Had even convinced myself there was a certain quixotic romance in such a gesture. What folly this appeared, now that all hopes of reconciliation had once again receded.

I couldn't help but recall the winter mornings in Fishers Meadows with a wistful nostalgia. It was at this time of the year that the sun might rise to reveal a frost that sparkled across the playing fields or a dense white mist drifting up from the river to hang like a fallen cloud. *Never say never.* The phrase had caused a rush of blood to my head—and in my impatience I had been tactless. It was surely only to be expected that Annie should be so protective of her traumatized son.

I paced the flat a great deal during this desolate period, noting the carpet stains and the box to catch cockroaches that protruded from behind the radiator. How I longed to find the pristinely folded hand towel rumpled by her careless hand. To return from work to share the minor triumphs and petty frustrations of the day before retiring to bed soothed by her warm presence beside me and her soft breath in the darkness if I woke.

Then one evening, as I sat brooding over a bottle of wine on this new setback, a notion of how I might remedy matters unexpectedly came to me. A notion that still, when I reviewed it the next morning, struck me as distinctly promising.

* * *

The woman who opened the door was in her sixties and dressed in a *salwar kameez*.

"Is Mr. Verdi here?" I asked.

The woman shook her head, explaining that her husband was away for a few days on business.

"It's just that he recently helped me out when I was in a bit of a fix. Gave me a lift with all my things and even found me somewhere to stay." My hands were pressed together in what I hoped might be an appropriate greeting. "I had a proposal I wanted to put to him. As a small thank-you."

She was nodding and smiling. "I know exactly who you are," she said and, offering a bow of welcome, opened the door wide enough to admit me. "I often see you pass by when I am working on my allotment."

As I stepped across the threshold, her glance fell anxiously on my shoes, and I at once bent to remove them. With my feet sinking into the deep pile of the carpet I followed her through into the sitting room, where she gestured to one of the sofas, before taking the other for herself. Though the layout of the house was an exact replica of Annie's, the presentation throughout offered a startling contrast in every other way. For it had the immaculate luster of a showroom, with arrangements of artificial flowers set here and there, giving the impression that it was seldom used. I was just about to make my proposal when she rose again.

"You must excuse me. My back is very bad at the moment," she explained apologetically, moving to a formal high-backed dining chair and settling herself with care.

Behind her head hung a large gilt-framed studio portrait in which she and her husband stood beside their adult son, who, like his father, wore a neat turban. At their feet sat five small grandsons, all in identical turbans too. Mistaking my brief glance for interest, she at once lit up.

"My son studied first at Cambridge, then Harvard," she told me, her reticence overridden by the rush of maternal pride. "Now he is vice president of a pharmaceutical company in Boston."

She fixed her eyes upon her lap, only allowing herself to look up once she had restored her self-effacing demeanor.

"Such wonderful news about your son! Barbara knocked on our door to tell us. You and your wife must be over the moon."

We were never married, nor was Dan my son, I might have said, discomfited by her assumption that our lives were as orderly as her own. And so much for Barbara's promise of discretion. Mrs. Verdi was watching me with a grave kindliness.

"Well, as you can imagine, the past two weeks have been a tremendous roller coaster. But now things are beginning to settle down again, Dan needs something to keep him out of mischief until his return to school. It just occurred to me that you or your husband might have some odd jobs you—"

"Oh yes!" She was already nodding with girlish enthusiasm. "Since I hurt my back, I have fallen behind with so many things. Perhaps your boy could help prepare my allotment for the winter? I would be most grateful."

Even as we rose to our feet and shook hands, I was already constructing the message to Annie. This opportunity to foster Dan's citizenship would surely prove irresistible.

Just as I had hoped, my text message drew a speedy and affirmative response. Then twenty minutes later, another one came, announcing that she had now spoken to Mrs. Verdi and arranged for Dan to begin work the very next day.

Eager to discover how things now stood between us, I stopped by unannounced on my way home from work the following evening. Annie was on the phone when she opened the door, but indicated with a nod and a distracted smile that I should come in. I followed her into the kitchen and stood waiting as she wound up the conversation.

"Well, I'm delighted!" she was saying. "I can't tell you how heartwarming that is to hear."

She was wearing her yoga gear again. Yoga! Another aspect of the old Annie I had entirely forgotten.

"That was Mrs. Verdi," she said, putting the phone down. "So pleased with all Dan's work today. Honestly, you should have seen him this morning. Off he went with the spade and hoe I'd found in the shed, looking thoroughly fed up about the whole thing. No lie-in. No Game Boy. He was not in the least bit amused, I can tell you. But he came home this evening so transformed! Said Mrs. Verdi had given him twenty pounds and a key to the allotments so that he could just come and go as he pleased until the job was done. Then he wolfed down an enormous supper before going upstairs to collapse. You are so clever to have thought of it. I really can't thank you enough."

She eyed me thoughtfully, appearing to weigh something inwardly, and realizing she was about to share a shy confidence of some kind, I arranged my face to receive it.

"I've got another bit of good news for you too." She smiled. An agreeable vision rose in my mind's eye of the two of us eating dinner at the kitchen table, conversing with all the familiar intimacy of old. "But before I tell you, would you give me your honest opinion about something?"

"Of course."

She took up a sheaf of loose papers from the dresser and set them before me on the table. Scanning them quickly, I saw that they were pen-and-ink drawings depicting what I could only presume were characters from a science-fiction comic of some kind.

"I took the opportunity to tidy Dan's room while he was out—and there they were."

They were executed in a detailed and competent hand, though they were evidently either copied or traced.

"I really think they've got something," she said, reaching out to align them. "But you're the expert. What do you think?"

"Most striking," I answered carefully.

When Dan got home that evening, he had been a bit put out to discover that she had been looking through his things, Annie said. But later, over supper, the conversation had led quite readily to the possibility of pursuing a GCSE in art, and before she knew it he was agreeing that if a suitable school could be found, he would be perfectly willing to start after Christmas.

"I realized how easily we could gloss over all those lost years. I simply need to say that ill health has severely disrupted his schooling. After all, that isn't, strictly speaking, a lie, is it?"

I nodded, gratified.

"So you see," she continued, her eyes alive with triumph, "little by little we *are getting there*."

On the doorstep, she kissed me fondly on the cheek. "Oh, by the way—I almost forgot," she added in a rush as I was turning to go. "Rachel would be thrilled if you would spend Christmas Day here. I've only just realized how close it's all getting."

"Let me check my diary and get back to you," I replied, in the vain hope that humor would disguise my unalloyed joy.

Later that night, buoyed by a new and agreeable glow, I slipped easily into sleep, only to wake some while later with a start, that odd troubled feeling still lurking at the edge of my thoughts. Had I not dispensed with it, after all? How these redundant habits of mind persisted. I got up, found some remnants of vodka in the freezer, and downed the dregs before retiring again—this time to sleep soundly until morning.

* * *

Midway through a meeting at the National Portrait Gallery the following day, Annie's name flashed up on my mobile. Muttering my apologies to assembled colleagues, I stepped at once into the corridor.

"You'll never guess," Annie announced in a singsong voice as if we were playing a party game. I waited. "Dan has just gone out with a friend!"

"A friend?" I repeated a little testily, conscious that our conversation might be audible through the door.

"A friend," she laughed merrily. "And a rather pretty one at that. Do you remember that note the police found in Dan's safe? The one from a girl in his class inviting him to go to the park after school?"

"Yes," I said, "I dimly recall it."

Apparently, the author of the note had just turned up on their doorstep—a sweet-faced black girl with a cascade of ringlets who introduced herself as Shania, before explaining that she had just heard of Dan's return and wanted to say hello.

Her effect on Dan when he came to the door had been remarkable, Annie went on. His eyes had lit up when he saw her, while Shania responded in kind with winsome smiles, twisting her hair coquettishly through her fingers. Perhaps there was some kudos in knowing this boy with his extraordinary story. Or perhaps it was only that she had retained her soft spot for him over the years. It had been charming to witness the pair of them chatting with such studied breeziness, while clearly so mutually taken with each other.

Annie had urged the girl to come in, but they insisted they were quite happy where they were. Eventually, though, Dan had announced that they were going to walk to the river, and Annie watched them set off with a funny wistful feeling—aware that she was witnessing a small rite of passage. Even as we spoke, she confessed with a tight little laugh, she was hovering at the kitchen window, anxiously awaiting their return.

9

The next weekend when I came to visit, I found the house in darkness, save for the chinks of light that spilled about the edges of the closed blind, making a brightly lit frame of the kitchen window. I stood in the street as twilight deepened, listening to the sound of their muted conversation through the glass. Now and then came a merry laugh. It was the bitter cold that roused me from my reverie, and when I rang the bell, it took some minutes for someone to come to the door. There was a flicker at the spy hole. Then the door opened a little way, held fast by the burglar chain. An eye blinked at child's height. Disappeared again. Then the scrabbling sound of the chain being slid free. At last the door swung open to reveal Rachel. She stepped past me, peeping cautiously out into the close, first one way, then the other, before urgently beckoning me in.

"A man came. A reporter. Said he'd heard rumors Dan was back." She spoke in a theatrical whisper. I looked behind me, but the close was definitely empty, the line of distant poplars slowly swaying against the darkening sky. I stepped into the hall.

"Mum went ballistic."

"I bet she did."

"Told him she'd never heard anything so far-fetched in her entire life." Rachel's eyes were scouring mine, her voice still a whisper. "Mum doesn't want Dan to know, so don't say anything." She slid the chain back into its slot. "We're making a Christmas cake. Come and see."

The kitchen smelled of brown sugar and nutmeg, underscored by the smoky sweetness of black treacle. Annie, midway through measuring sherry into the bowl, greeted me with a distracted smile, while sitting beside her Dan was flicking raisins into the air and throwing his head back to catch them. At each attempt, Rachel laughed with delight—and when he finally succeeded, neatly ingesting the raisin with an audible click of his teeth, she clapped her hands together and danced about the kitchen. Evidently, much had changed since our walk across the meadows. Was this all it took to inspire such hero worship?

I looked at Annie. In the old days, Dan's foolish antics would surely have made her impatient, but today she remained immersed in her measuring and stirring, an indulgent half smile hovering about her lips. I eyed the lone empty chair, and since no invitation was forthcoming sat myself down anyway, surveying the three of them with determined cheerfulness.

Rachel and Dan took it in turns to stir the ingredients, and at once there was another outbreak of silly giggling as they pretended to spatter each other with the gooey mess.

"Don't beat," Annie admonished gently. "*Fold.*" She demonstrated the twisting reflex of the wrist.

"Annie tells me you're going back to school after Christmas," I said to Dan in a tone I hoped jovial enough to match the prevailing mood.

"Worse luck." He was smiling boldly from under the sweep of his fringe. "I said I was fine just chilling out at home. But she weren't having none of it." From behind the smile I formed the disconcerting impression that he was coolly sizing me up. Then with his eyes still upon me, he seized the bottle of sherry and offered a toast, "*Cheers, Big Ears!*" before swinging it to his lips and brazenly gulping down a great mouthful. I watched transfixed.

"Hey! That's quite enough of that, young man." Annie plucked the bottle good-naturedly from his grasp, while Dan wiped his lips on the back of his hand, exhaling with gusto.

"I'm not a kid anymore, you know."

She smiled dotingly. "I know. But neither are you yet quite an adult. However . . ."

Rising swiftly to her feet, she went to the cupboard and brought back four little wineglasses that she set down before us.

"We do have something rather special to celebrate."

She filled each one with a tot of the sherry.

"To Dan!" she said, raising her glass to him, and the three of us followed suit, making a cheery clinking sound.

"Do you know the story of the Prodigal Son?" I asked him.

Once again Dan's amused expression rested on me.

"'We should make merry and be glad for this thy brother was dead, and is alive again; was lost and is found.'"

A smile was slowly spreading across his face.

"It's a story from the New Testament," I went on. "It just struck me that it bore a certain resemblance to your own, that's all. Though I seem to recall that it was a fatted calf with which his family celebrated, rather than a glass of sherry."

Dan shook his head and looked at Annie for help. "He's lost me."

She laughed, glancing impishly at me. "I'm afraid Julian has always had a tendency to talk in riddles."

After a while I left them to it and wandered restlessly about the house. The place seemed to have shrunk, each room more airless and overheated than the last. Or perhaps I was coming down with something. I certainly felt a little out of sorts today. I stood in the doorway of Rachel's room. The rows of books and the doll's house I had given her for her birthday, all as spick-and-span as ever, while Annie's room just across the landing displayed its habitual disarray, clothes strewn about the floor, her silk kimono flung across the unmade bed. Downstairs, the phone rang, Annie's answering voice just audible.

"Soon," she was saying. "Very soon, I promise." Then a

pause as she listened. "Honestly, the moment he's ready for visitors, you'll be the first to know."

Dan's attic room, when I reached the top floor and gingerly pushed upon the door, was the only one that had altered. Inside, its former order had vanished under an assortment of discarded clothes and debris. There was a pungent musky smell in the air, and on the wall various posters of buxom girls in provocative poses. Beside the door lay a pair of brand-new trainers several shoe sizes larger than my own.

It was as I passed the bathroom on my way downstairs again that my eye fell upon Dan's razor lying casually discarded beside the sink in the bathroom, almost exactly in the spot my own had only so recently lain. Good God! Did a boy of fifteen really need to shave? And there lying next to it was his toothbrush. I had stood precisely here that grim day the forensic investigator returned to collect a sample of Dan's DNA. I could still picture him sealing Dan's toothbrush into the Ziploc plastic bag before securing it in his leather briefcase and snapping off his gloves. How Annie's heart must have plummeted as she absorbed the implications of his assignment.

Stepping forward, I picked the brush up, weighing it thoughtfully. It had been the first inkling that a search for a missing child might become at some point a murder inquiry. An impression only compounded when shortly afterwards the police asked for permission to obtain his dental records too. How odd and unexpected each new twist of Dan's unfolding story had proved to be. I put the brush back exactly as I had found it, a shudder passing through me.

In the kitchen I found him plundering the fridge. I paused in the doorway to watch as he set about assembling a sandwich: a hunk of bread smothered first with peanut butter, followed by a sprinkling of cornflakes, topped by a squirt of tomato ketchup. The old Dan had moved like a sullen shadow about the house, but this physically mature incarnation commanded the room. He was shirtless, and his tracksuit pants hung low enough to expose a wide expanse of underpant elastic in the style so de rigueur among his generation. I saw why Annie had thought of a statue when she looked upon him sleeping, for his muscular physique might indeed have been formed by the skillful bite of a sculptor's chisel.

Oblivious to my presence, he stood at the open door of the fridge again, contemplating what more he might pillage, all the while scratching languidly at the flat expanse of belly just above his crotch, and yawning noisily as if his culinary exertions thus far had exhausted him. Then he took out a carton of orange juice, upending it into his mouth before discharging a loud belch with such unseemly relish that, unable to endure it any longer, I was starting forward to indignantly reprimand him when Annie appeared at my elbow.

"Goodness me, you'll eat us out of house and home!" she exclaimed, sounding more gratified than reproachful, and hastening forward to cut his grotesque creation in two before sliding it deftly onto a plate.

At long last Rachel was ready to set forth across the meadows. But it was dark now, and such a biting wind came from the river that we had barely turned the corner of the close before she began to drag her feet and complain at the cold. Very soon, to her evident relief, I relented and we turned for home.

"You and Dan appear to be getting on rather well now," I observed, though she only shrugged as she strode ahead.

"He's actually really funny when you get to know him," she acknowledged carelessly.

On our return, Rachel got ready for bed while I unearthed the copy of *Pilgrim's Progress* we had been reading together before Dan's return interrupted my weekly visits. I tucked her into bed, and she curled beside me in her customary way, stifling a dainty yawn. Very soon the two of us were once again immersed. Christian and Hopeful had just passed out of the Land of Beulah into the Valley of the Shadow, and the landscape all about them had changed to one full of foreboding.

I had paused for dramatic effect when I heard a sound—the smallest sigh from just outside on the landing—and, looking round the door, discovered Dan sitting there cross-legged. His head was tilted against the wall, and he was apparently so deeply absorbed in the story that he started violently at the sight of me. When I exclaimed in surprise,

Rachel at once called out for him to join us, and after a moment's hesitation he came to sit with an awkward formality at the end of her bed.

I read on, a little self-consciously now, though very soon the melodic rhythm of the prose had cast its spell again, and a complete stillness held the room. Once or twice I glanced with covert bemusement at Dan. How fruitlessly I had tried to introduce him to the joys of literature in the old days. I read for far longer than normal, until my throat was dry and aching, and once or twice I became aware of Annie coming to stand in the doorway, only to tiptoe away again, loath to break their enchantment. By the time Christian and Hopeful came to Final River, my voice was so diminished I suggested we resume the next time I came, only for Rachel to protest with such vigor—and Dan to look so crestfallen—that eventually I relented and continued on until the very end.

When I had uttered the final sentence, I shut the book with a pleasing clap. It was Rachel who broke the hush, stretching with a noisy yawn. Then Dan stood up in a daze, walking as if the room sloped steeply to the door.

"Here. Why don't you borrow it?" I said. "You can go back to the beginning and catch up on the parts you've missed."

He turned and took the book, surveying it uncertainly before studying me with care as if to discern my intention. I looked at him more closely.

"You *can* still remember how to read, can't you?"

A little jolt of indignation went through him. "Course!"

He wet his lips. I had a dim impression of Rachel looking on with a shocked expression.

"Perhaps you would tell me what is written on the front there then?"

His glance raked the letters, while his mouth tried for different consonants, an unmistakable flush of color rising in his cheeks.

"Just the title will do . . ."

His eyes snapped at me. Then he thrust the book back into my hands and strode out. I heard him take the stairs two at a time to his room.

In the kitchen I found Annie in an apron clearing the remnants of cake making. She was polishing the worktop, reaching out on the tips of her toes to sweep the cloth to and fro. Judging by an uncharacteristic gleam in the room, she had worked her way about the kitchen with some zeal.

What was it she had said when she was discussing his return to school? *I realized how easily we could gloss over all those lost years*. There were already a few Christmas cards arranged on the dresser, and I took them down in turn, making a pretense of reading them while I experimented with a tentative inquiry about the police. Twice I opened my mouth to embark on it—and twice I closed it again, silenced by a disquieting vision of Annie's pinched expression as she closed the door on me, of wandering my wretched flat in an egg-stained dressing gown, the phone once again silent, my text messages unanswered. This latest alliance between us had been hard won. Anything that broke the unspoken terms of my probation was going to need careful forethought.

She chatted on about her plans for Christmas, and once or twice I nodded mechanically. It was perfectly obvious she hadn't the slightest inclination to investigate the mysteries Dan trailed in his wake. She had made her decision—I could see that now. Left to her own devices she was evidently happy to leave things exactly as they were.

The wind was buffeting the front door as I buttoned my coat, while Annie bent to load the dishwasher in the kitchen. I was not about to desert her in her hour of need. She was a decent woman who had found herself in extraordinary circumstances. Though she might not know it, she was in need of an emissary to discreetly set about unraveling this puzzle on her behalf—and thus resolved, I went through to bid her good night.

8

When I rang the next morning to announce that I had a spare ticket for the Christmas carol concert at St. Martin-in-the-Fields and was hoping Dan would join me, Annie's first reaction was to laugh.

"Dan? Go to a carol concert with you!" There was a pause. "Well, I suppose he might like it," she said doubtfully. Then another pause. "How would he get there?"

"Well, I thought I might come and collect him after work."

She said nothing, immersed in a tussle I could imagine only too well—favorably disposed towards anything culturally improving while loath to relinquish him unchaperoned into my hands.

"So you only have two tickets then?"

"Sadly."

There was a pause.

"It's terribly sweet of you, Julian, but I'm afraid it's just still too early for him to be out and about without me."

* * *

I watched with a heavy heart as the three of them crossed from Trafalgar Square, weaving their way through the lines of static traffic. From a distance Annie gave the impression of guiding Dan rather as a sheepdog might, for he was walking in a conspicuously leisurely fashion, trailing his feet at every step. I greeted them with as much good cheer as I could contrive, though Annie appeared distracted while Dan hung back with a stony expression. It was only Rachel who came forward to greet me and took my hand as we joined the throng of people queuing at the doors.

Inside the church there were rows of candles burning along the window ledges, their light catching the bottle glass of the great arched windows in a series of brilliant squares. We found seats near the front, and Dan slumped into his place, folding his arms and propping his feet on the bar of the pew before him. While the choir sang, I let my eyes roam idly across the vaulted ceiling and on over the Baroque colonnades and high lectern. Already the music was calming the agitation in me. At first Dan was fidgety and restless, but even he appeared to be succumbing to the music's soothing enchantment, his hands lying loosely folded in his lap and his head crooked to one side. When we all rose to sing the first carol, he was the only member of the congregation to remain seated. Yet I could discern no truculence in his expression. Indeed, I formed the distinct impression, from my covert inspection, that he had fallen into a deep reverie.

It was in the second half of the concert, when the congregation rose once more, to sing "Silent Night," that Annie gripped my wrist. She was smiling, despite the fact her eyes brimmed with tears, and she made a discreet gesture for me to look at Dan. I turned to see that, though his head still rested on his hand, and his posture still conveyed the impression that he was only begrudgingly filling time, he was now singing. Indeed, his light baritone, just audible among the general rumble, was undeniably melodious.

"And I've always thought he was tone-deaf!" Annie whispered hoarsely in my ear.

At the end of the concert Dan hunched back into himself as we shuffled out among the crowds, and only shrugged in a noncommittal manner when I asked if he had enjoyed the evening. Annie kept darting bright glances towards him.

"You sang so beautifully, darling," she said twice, over the bobbing shoulders of the departing congregation, fruitlessly attempting to catch his eye.

Rachel turned confidingly to me. "There was a bit of a row because Dan didn't want to come."

"Didn't he indeed?"

Unable to resist this, Dan spun round, glaring accusingly at Annie.

"So *she*—she said she'd bin me Game Boy if I didn't."

The traffic roared beside us, and on the far side of the road the Norwegian Christmas tree sparkled in Trafalgar Square. Smiling in tender reproach, Annie reached out to brush Dan's hair from his eyes, but he flinched away from her, sucking his teeth in annoyance. At once she busied herself hunting out a handkerchief in her bag, and I half expected her to moisten it with her tongue before bearing down on him again, so determined did she appear to bestow some kind of maternal gesture. But he had already turned his back and begun to kick at a raised paving stone while she eyed him reproachfully as she used the handkerchief to blow her nose instead. There was something so self-conscious about this scene, something so patently contrived in her efforts to achieve an effect of spontaneity that I couldn't but think, with a little cold thump, I might be watching a play.

We were about to go our separate ways when Annie, belatedly remembering her manners, turned to thank me for the evening before hurrying after Dan. I watched them go, weighted by foreboding. Now Rachel came hastily forward to embrace me. "Please don't look so sad," she said. Then Annie had called her name, and she too was gone.

7

I picked Annie's message up the following afternoon as I emerged from the underground at Bond Street. She wanted to thank me again for the concert, she said. It had been a real treat. How full of new surprises Dan was turning out to be! She was only sorry he'd been so surly and ungracious about the whole thing—though she thought I'd be pleased to hear that he'd just woken up in a rather better frame of mind and set off for the allotments with uncharacteristic enthusiasm. Much as she hated to admit it, it was rather nice to have the house all to . . .

I didn't bother to listen to the rest. Already a cab had responded to my urgent wave, swinging from the other side of the street to pull up beside me with a purr. The roads were empty, every light in our favor. Before I knew it we had reached Fishers Meadows. The realization that I might finally be closing in upon him had filled me with such a fever of anticipation that it was only once I had paid my fare and turned for the allotments that I realized I had neglected to form even the sketchiest of plans.

As I approached the gates, there were bonfires burning all over the allotments, filling the air with an acrid aroma. Russian vine weighted the perimeter fence, half screening the interior in a dense tangle of foliage, but when I bent to peer through the gaps, there was no sign of Dan at work anywhere. I saw an elderly man tending a burning brazier and then beyond him, at the far side—my heart gave a little leap—there he was, sitting outside Mrs. Verdi's shed, meditatively puffing on a cigarette. Though I called a greeting he appeared not to hear, and I hastened on to the main gates, which stood ajar and swung open to reveal a world within a world. Here and there, little figures bent over their patches of land, dwarfed by the dense vegetation that, despite the advance of winter, still sprouted exuberantly on every side.

Dan nodded affably enough at my approach, his eyes narrowing as he drew on the cigarette.

"Annie would have a fit if she saw you."

He shrugged, letting the smoke out in a slow coiling plume.

"Yeah, well, that's why I like it here," he said. "No one to give me any grief, is there?"

Up close, Mrs. Verdi's shed was no more than a wooden frame covered by plastic sheeting with a few parched tomato plants struggling for life inside. I heard my name and turned to find Mrs. Verdi hobbling towards us, her arms full of freshly cut rhubarb, her long plait swinging at her back.

"He's worked very hard, this boy of yours. And I think we're all but done now." She smiled appreciatively at him, and the three of us surveyed the newly cleared beds. I turned back to Dan.

"Don't suppose," I said casually, "you fancy a quick stroll to the park and back? It's been such a lovely day, and we'll just catch the last of it if we hurry."

To my great relief, he rose at once to his feet, grinding the remainder of the cigarette underfoot.

"We won't be long," I said to Mrs. Verdi, who nodded gravely and settled herself with care in the chair Dan had vacated, sitting bolt upright like a sentinel at her post.

There was an exceptional clarity of light, as if the air had been washed clean and the rows of houses we passed were no more than painted scenery. Even though it was already late afternoon, patches of frost still glittered where the warmth of the sun had yet to fall. So here we were. At last alone! Anxious not to set things off on the wrong note, I played for time with an observation about the weather before an uneasy silence settled between us. We passed Dan's old school, though he didn't so much as glance towards it. A little farther on and we had stepped through the handsome stuccoed gates of the park.

"What a wealth of hidden talents you have revealed in

these past few weeks." I chose my words with care. "First an artist. Now a singer."

That wary glance again, as if uncertain whether he was being mocked, and instead of answering he fixed his eyes diffidently on the ground. All about us the shadows were lengthening, the sun slanting sideways across the lawn.

"So how's it all going?"

"All right, I suppose."

"I imagine the past few weeks must have been something of a roller coaster."

"How d'you mean?" With a swift and appraising glance, his eyes darted towards me and away.

"Well, finding yourself suddenly in the bosom of your family like that. Back with your mother—your sister—*once more in your home.*"

"Yeh." He walked deep in thought. "To tell you the truth, it's totally done me head in."

We came to the bridge and climbed its steep incline, walking in step.

"Surely, after all this time, some memories must at last be stirring?"

He shook his head, frowning.

"We watched these home movies the other day, and I was like, no way," he said. "I never had no hairstyle that bad. I never wore those clothes! I was like, 'Check out the little posh kid.' Playing cricket in the garden!"

Though I attempted to laugh, I found nerves had got the better of me. If the Dan who had vanished had been an enigma to me, this young man walking with a young primate's easy swagger was an altogether more daunting prospect.

We were skirting the lake, the water a blackened mirror today, fallen leaves resting on its dark surface like a tabletop. We paused for a moment beside the great willow tree that bent so gracefully to meet its twin.

"Your mother tells a story about how she lost you here when you were a little boy. One minute you were there; the next thing she knew, you'd vanished," I began, a new tack fortuitously presenting itself. "She said she remembered promising the powers above that she would never ask for anything again if you could only be returned safe and sound to her. It was every mother's worst nightmare . . ."

He kept glancing towards me.

"And then what happened?" he asked impatiently.

"You unexpectedly appeared again! As magically as you'd gone, you were back. You must have lost your bearings and cycled off in the wrong direction."

Dan exhaled with an odd wily chuckle, nodding as he took this in. I saw to my dismay that we had almost completed our circuit of the lake and were once again nearing the park gates, the sun just touching the treetops.

"And then it happened again," I went on in as neutral a voice as I could muster. "Only this time you were twelve. And this time it wasn't twenty minutes you were gone, but three years."

The quacking of the ducks sounded unnaturally loud

now. We walked in silence, still keeping perfect time with each other, the only sound the crunch of stones beneath our feet. I risked a quick glance, but Dan's profile gave nothing away. A small child on a bicycle shot from round the corner, passing between us like some ghostly incarnation of the incident I had just recounted. Close behind him came the child's smiling mother, murmuring her apologies as she brushed past us. And now, without warning, the pavement was thronged with home-bound schoolchildren who streamed along the path towards us, a clamor of shouts and taunts rising and falling between them.

"Oi! You wasteman cuntface!" One of the boys was attempting to beat another about the head with a pair of muddy football boots that he held by the laces, only the howls of laughter from their companions distinguishing it as horseplay rather than assault.

"Look a mi felis. Mi look like me jokin?" the other boy shrieked, making a wild lunge for his assailant.

Though the flood of children had momentarily submerged us, Dan remained deep in thought.

"So you met your mother at the station," I prompted, "with your sister standing beside her—and it is as if you are looking at two complete strangers?"

He nodded slowly in confirmation.

"You are driven to the house in which you have lived for twelve years—you walk through the front door—yet it's as if you've never set foot in it before?"

"Sort of . . ."

"Sort of?"

"I mean yes. Apart from a . . . a kind of . . ." He sniffed ruminatively, gesturing at the air about his nose as if evoking a half-remembered smell. "I can't put it into words."

The noise of the children had passed away, and the quiet twittering of birdsong seemed to open a new chapter of possibility between us.

"Well, you must try. You must make every effort. For I have to tell you quite frankly that I am deeply uneasy about the events of the past few weeks. Unless you can begin to fill in the gaps, I can see no option but to call in some kind of professional help. Are you absolutely certain you are unable to offer any explanation as to where you may have been or why it was you went?"

"I've gone over and over it in me head—trying and trying—but . . . I'm telling you, it's all just a blank."

I saw we were hard upon the gates now, the street only moments away. From high in the trees came the piercing shriek of parakeets, and I caught a quick flash of green and red as a score of them darted overhead. We stepped out onto the street again.

"Perhaps someone kidnapped you?" I asked desperately.

"*Kidnapped* me?" He sounded astonished.

"Did someone take you against your will?"

"I . . . I think . . ." He was frowning deeply now, as if something at last stirred, his eyes appearing to roam across an interior space. We were passing his old school again, the pavement now teeming with homeward-bound children.

"School had ended. You said good-bye to Obi. Just here. You must have been standing almost exactly on this spot."

"Right here?" He stopped, and the hordes of children parted to flow around us. "I said good-bye."

"You said good-bye, then you set off on your bike."

"I set off on me bike. Yeah. It was freezing, I remember that."

"You remember!"

"I get down to the lights at the end of the road . . ." He turned to glance towards them. "I'm feeling really messed up . . ."

His brow was tightly knitted, as if a host of bewildering thoughts moved elusively to and fro, before a sudden anguished shout caused us both to jump in alarm. Annie was at the far end of the street, trotting towards us.

"*There you are!*" she was calling frantically as she ran. "There you are."

I seized his arm. "What? What was it that had so upset you?"

"I'm feeling messed up because . . ." he tried, before faltering once more, distracted by another cry from Annie.

"*Because?*"

"Because I've realized I'm not needed no more. That it's better for everyone if I—"

But by then Annie had burst upon us.

"I've been calling and calling your phone!" Though her face was pale, she was already forcing some semblance of a smile, and smoothing her windblown hair. She stood trying to catch her breath.

"Mrs. Verdi said I'd find you here." She threw me a brief reproachful glare that melted the instant she turned to Dan. She took him by the arm. "It's getting dark and your tea's ready, darling."

They turned for Fishers Meadows, leaving me to follow on behind, and we made our way with difficulty through the milling, shrieking children.

"Hey there!" A pretty girl was waving animatedly from the other side of the road, causing her companions to turn one by one to scrutinize us.

Annie nodded in her direction. "Hello, Shania."

Shania whispered something conspiratorially to her friends and from among their ranks came first an admiring whistle or two, followed by a pattering of applause.

"He came back from the dead!" one of the taller boys called out in the melodramatic tones of a cinema trailer. Dan acknowledged his audience with a sideways smirk, before continuing on his way with a newly jaunty swagger.

At the house, Dan went inside and Annie turned quickly.

"Well?"

"What?"

"I suppose you've been busily plying him with questions?"

"I . . . I may have attempted to draw him out a little."

"And?" she pressed.

I paused. "You must talk to him," I said at last. "It seems

a story of sorts is beginning to emerge. I'd very much like to hear what you make of it."

But she only nodded in a slow, thoughtful fashion, before going inside and closing the door.

When I got home I sat down at the computer. What a very odd business this amnesia was. Was it really possible for someone to forget so much? Surely some fundamental experiences were etched too deeply within us to be lost for long.

I trawled inconclusively for a while, until at last I stumbled upon something: *When a child learns to ride a bicycle, he makes two sets of memories: one is explicit memory, which records things such as the color of the bike and the elation of riding unassisted. Implicit memory, on the other hand, notes the body mechanics required to ride the bike. Even when explicit memories fail, implicit ones remain.* I paced the room for a while. *Even when explicit memories fail, implicit ones remain.* Quite what light this information cast on Dan and his predicament, I couldn't yet tell, but I stored it carefully away nonetheless.

6

It was late the following day when Annie called to ask if I would come to dinner.

"Have you spoken to him then?" I asked.

"Yes—yes, I have." The emotion in her voice told its own story. "And your conversation in the park has definitely triggered something. I'll tell you everything when I see you."

I washed and showered with due gravity, before putting on a freshly laundered shirt and securing each button in slow sequence. I combed my hair in the mirror, pausing for a moment to consider my reflection. The things that habitually pleased me—the firm jawline, the only marginally diminished head of hair—were tonight superseded by the apprehension in the eyes that met mine.

For the first hour after I arrived, Annie was distracted by the children and unusually shrill and short-tempered with them both. At length, after I had helped settle Rachel, and

Dan had been disentangled from his PlayStation and slunk upstairs, we were able to begin our meal. With the room in semidarkness, and the table lit only by the pendant lamp, it was a situation that at any other time might have gladdened my heart. Yet I could scarcely conceal my impatience. We passed the steaming dishes to and fro, and I poured us both a glass of wine, waiting in a quiet agony of suspense.

"So?" I prompted at last, unable to bear it any longer. But instead of answering she only pushed her food about her plate. After a moment a glistening tear appeared, quickly followed by another.

"Well, I asked him quite directly why it was he went that day," she finally began. "And he said . . . he said he wasn't sure, but that maybe, because we were getting married, he had felt he was in the way. That it would be better for everyone if he just left us to it." She wiped away more tears. "It totally floored me. That he could ever have got hold of such an idea. That I could ever have allowed such a misunderstanding to arise."

She stopped to collect herself for a moment, fishing in her sleeve for a tissue before blowing her nose. "But the truth is that I *was* distracted. I can't deny it. We were very caught up in each other, weren't we?" She frowned. "It's so hard to disentangle it all now. I mean, I can't deny there were things I turned a blind eye to—petty tensions between the two of you I should have faced up to at the time."

Through the window beyond her, a gust of wind brought down a flurry of leaves that caught the orange arc of the streetlamp, and fell flashing and pirouetting like bright cinders in the darkness.

"He said he dimly remembered abandoning his bicycle on the high street before taking the first bus that came along. When he got off, he no longer had any idea where he was. It was as if he'd cast himself adrift."

Quite unconsciously, her agitated fingers traced and skimmed the grain of the tabletop. She drained her glass, and I opened a new bottle from which to replenish it.

"He said he wished he knew what happened after that. He only knows that since he's been back, he's been plagued by nightmares."

"What kind of nightmares?"

"In his dreams he's always moving from place to place. Always searching for somewhere warm to sleep, or something to eat. Sometimes in the dream feral children appear out of the shadows, and he never knows whether they are going to rob or befriend him. He said he often wakes in a cold sweat of terror."

"Jesus . . ."

She looked at me, nodding slowly. "I know. I told him the hardest thing was to understand how three years could have passed without anyone ever challenging him or offering to help. He was only twelve—still just a little boy when he went. He must often have been frightened, I said." Still the tears fell, though she pressed on, angrily brushing them away with a dismissive hand. "I said that frankly it beggared belief. *Three years!*" Her voice cracked. "I told him that in my darkest hours I sometimes wondered whether he wasn't deliberately keeping something back. Surely there must be more to the story—someone who took him in? Someone who perhaps prevented him from leaving? But he just kept saying he couldn't remember. I said I knew all about the exploitation of children on the streets. That he wasn't to feel ashamed if something untoward had happened—that it wouldn't have been his fault. What was it, I kept pressing, that could possibly have prevented him from returning? But he just got more and more upset. He said I could ask all the questions I liked, but the truth was he simply had no more answers."

A silence fell between us.

"So there's still more to come."

"Yes, there's still much more to come." She nodded. "Though I have a feeling that the rest may follow very quickly now."

"I'm afraid you're going to have to be very brave, Annie."

She sighed, falling into a deep reverie while I refilled our glasses, then after a moment she stood up and went to put some music on, the plangent lilt of Van Morrison at once softening the tension in the room. Then she blew her nose and dried her eyes, apparently resolving to rally.

"You've been amazing in the past few weeks," she said, resuming her seat. "Please don't think I haven't appreciated it."

She swept her hair back from her face and rested her chin on her hands.

"I'm sorry if I've been a bit overprotective at times." That pearly smile—like a flash of sunshine. "You've done your best to try and befriend him, and all I've done is get in your way."

"I'm perfectly accustomed to waiting in the wings by now."

"Are you?"

"Always ready for even the smallest crumbs that might fall from the high table."

"Poor you." She laughed ruefully, and her hand closed about mine. "We were an odd couple, I know. At first it was a relief that you were so different from David. It stopped me from being reminded of him, I suppose. Made me feel less disloyal." The almost imperceptible slurring of her words only infused this somehow with a maudlin tenderness.

"And then?"

"And then—I resented it and couldn't forgive you." Her mouth formed a little pout of regret. "I'm sorry. Really I am. I mean, despite your funny little ways, you're really very endearing." She was leaning towards me with a distinctly seductive expression, her head wobbling on her hand. "And you always saw something wonderful in me no one else did. I'll be forever grateful to you for that."

"I still think about you all the time, Annie. I'd do anything for you, you know that."

"Is this what you've been missing?" she whispered, pulling me to my feet and knocking my glasses sideways, her mouth on mine, quick fingers at my belt—in a flash the old Annie, the Annie of infinite mischief in my arms once more!

I felt as much as heard the sharp exhalation of her breath scorch my ear as I ran my hand across her buttocks and beneath her dress, not stopping till I had found a way over the top of her tights, hooking my fingers into the sides of her underwear with a confidence, a dexterity she appeared to find more irresistible than presumptuous. Evidently, alcohol had blurred the need for any rituals of foreplay, for she responded with a greedy relish, and I felt her hand between my legs as she twisted backwards into the hall, drawing me with her.

"Oh!" she sighed as we entwined like flailing teenagers. "*Oh*," she breathed again as we slid sideways along the wall, knocking three pictures in turn askew, from somewhere the faint tearing of fabric and the rattle of a falling button. Then the sitting room door gently gave way against our weight and we twisted backwards once again, tumbling heedlessly over the arm of the sofa, and into its cushioned embrace just a short free fall beyond.

5

When I opened my eyes the next morning, it was some moments before I could recall where I was. I slowly took in the faded sprigs of roses that scattered the wallpaper and the dressing table littered with cosmetics, as if someone had simply upended a bag there. I turned to press my face into the pillow, inhaling the fragrance of Annie, before stretching luxuriously. The smell of cooking bacon drifted up the stairs, and the distant shouts of a Saturday football game came from the playing fields beyond. Even the light that glimmered between the half-pulled curtains appeared to promise a morning of unusual loveliness. Perhaps it was really only now, I reflected, fondly stroking the familiar texture of the counterpane, when everything had been so thrown into jeopardy before being rescued at the eleventh hour, that I was truly ready for the hugger-mugger compromises of family life.

Annie was wearing the threadbare silk kimono she often

wore about the house. I paused in the doorway to admire the curve of her bare calves as she hovered at the cooker, the toes so elegantly tapered like fingers and the tantalizing way in which the sheen of the fabric implied the sinuous form beneath. I walked to her and threaded my arms about her waist, but she pulled away with a little laugh, her dark hair falling across one eye. "Julian, please! There are children present."

I turned to find Rachel demurely eating her breakfast and threw myself down beside her with a wink.

"My two most favorite girls in all the world!" But she only rolled her eyes and turned her shoulder to me.

"You're gross," she said with disdain.

It was later, after dropping Rachel off at her Saturday-morning drama class, that the idea came to me. A gift for Dan a Christmas present handsome enough to mark the end of old hostilities and the dawning of a new era. I parked Annie's car illegally on the high street and hastily made my purchase before heading for Fishers Meadows again. Perhaps it was presumptuous to describe it as home just yet, but for the first time the prevailing signs struck me as undeniably promising. The low winter sun shone full in my face, its dazzle intermittently blinding me as it came and went from behind the bare trees, and I drove with one hand outstretched to screen it, humming a fragment of a carol. When I recalled how all four of us had sung in unison at the concert, such a heady sensation of optimism swept through me it was as if elation alone was powering my very way forward.

At the house I slipped my shoes off in the hall and tossed my coat over the banister. The television was on in the sitting room, and when I put my head round the door, there was Dan, lying slumped in his customary manner, with a bowl of cereal propped on his chest.

"A very fine morning to you, young man! Where's your mother got to?"

It took him a moment to digest the question.

"Upstairs," he said eventually.

"Sleep all right?"

"Yup."

His eyes barely flickered from the screen. I went into the kitchen and stood looking out at the blue sky, humming contentedly. Mrs. Verdi passed by, raising a friendly hand, and I stood to attention, offering her a jaunty salute in return. If not now, when? I thought. I went back into the sitting room.

"Dan?"

His eyes remained locked on the screen. After a moment I clicked the television on to mute and went to sit beside him, clearing my throat.

"Dan."

At last his eyes slowly slid in my direction.

"It was good to have a chance to talk like that."

He was chewing the cereal, his mouth going round and round as if masticating hay.

"And I gather you've made more progress since then. Begun to fill in a few more gaps."

Now he was fishing something from between his teeth.

"Look. You've been through a lot—and it's important you remember I'm here for you, okay? You must feel free to call upon me as and when the need arises."

He nodded, his eyes already sliding back to the screen, and despite myself, the old feeling of exasperation was rising in me again.

"It occurred to me we might make another trip together some time—just the two of us."

He shrugged. "If you like."

I stood up. "Oh and by the way," I said, pausing in the doorway. "Step outside for a moment, would you? I've got something for you."

I put my coat back on and stood waiting for him in the hall. For a moment I thought he might not come, but then he appeared in the doorway, stretching and yawning.

"What's up?"

I threw open the front door. "Ta-da!"

Dan's eyes fixed upon the brand-new bicycle now tied to the fence, and I was gratified to observe that his mouth had fallen open.

"For me?"

"An early Christmas present. A bit premature, I know, but I thought, what the hell. Seize the day and all that."

"Wow. Cool. Thanks!"

He stepped towards it, entranced, running an admiring

hand along the saddle and across the handlebars while I bent to unlock the chain. It took a bit of struggling, but finally it sprang free.

"Go on then. Try it for size."

He straddled it with ease, sitting with an experimental bounce into the saddle, smiling at the resisting spring of the frame.

"Cool," he said again, in awe.

"It's as close a match to your father's as I could find."

I leaned forward and swung open the garden gate, gesturing to the road beyond.

"Why don't you take a spin?"

He screwed up his face doubtfully.

"Look." I took hold of the handlebars, guiding him firmly out onto the empty road, and he gingerly paddled his feet as we went. "You've got the street entirely to yourself."

He swallowed, glancing first at the road then back to me. For the first time it occurred to me that it was only too likely he hadn't ridden a bicycle since that fateful day.

"Been a while, hey?"

He licked his lips, nodding. Then made an impetuous lurching motion as if to set off, before immediately thinking better of it. We were standing so close, I could hear the rasp of his breath.

"You *can* do it," I said. "Indeed, I have it on good authority that it's the one thing in life one can never forget. The sense of balance is imprinted within you."

Dan nodded, and I heard his sharp inhalation before he

shot forward like a bird taking flight, moving at such speed that my hand, which had been resting on the small of his back, was left extended in midair as if in fond farewell. Yet almost at once both he and the machine skewed sideways, the back wheel sliding from underneath him, bringing both bike and boy crashing to the ground in a sprawl of limbs and oddly angled framework. I stood rooted to the spot. Without even acknowledging it to myself, I saw that I had set him a test. For some seconds the inescapable magnitude of what it revealed held me rooted to the spot.

I thought afterwards that it was his pride that was more hurt than anything. Certainly a cursory inspection of the bicycle suggested it remained surprisingly unscathed. Once I had helped him up and brushed him down, he limped slowly back to the house, leaving me to follow on with the bicycle and padlock it to the fence again. By the time I stepped back into the hall he had once more resumed his prone position in front of the television and was indolently flicking channels. I took the stairs two at a time.

On the landing, the ladder to the loft was down and the loft door ajar. I could hear the sound of boxes being dragged about above my head.

"Annie," I hissed urgently. "*Annie!*"

Standing at the foot of the ladder, I called her name several times more, until the thumps finally stopped and her face appeared, framed by the hatch.

"*What?*"

I made an urgent gesture for her to come down, and after a moment she did so, but slowly, encumbered by the box of Christmas decorations she carried under one arm. As she stepped from the bottom rung, she set the box down with care before brushing the dust from her hands and knees.

"Look." She lifted out a little homemade angel and held it spinning back and forth on its golden thread. "Isn't that just the most adorable thing you've ever seen?"

I beckoned her to come closer, but she swept her hair from her eyes with the back of her hand and straightened. "You look like you've just seen a ghost."

My head was full of stammers and prevarications, yet the sentence when it emerged was startlingly succinct.

"That boy downstairs—that boy isn't really Dan."

The little muscular contraction behind her eyes was almost imperceptible, yet I felt it like a kick. She moved slowly away from me. For a moment I thought she might fall, but as I reached out to steady her, she drew herself upright.

"I'm so sorry, Annie. More sorry than I can say. But I think the time for one of us to call the police is long overdue."

Her expression of incomprehension was rapidly giving way to one of disbelief.

"What . . . what *are* you talking about?"

Where to begin? *A gut feeling. Discrepancies in his appearance. The fact that his amnesia appeared to amount to little more than a smoke screen.* I could hear the rapid shallow rush of her breathing, and already I was regretting this impulsive assault on her hard-won happiness. Without proper forethought I was about to bring this house of cards about our ears.

For some moments our eyes remained locked; then, glancing down the stairs, she took me by the arm and propelled me into her bedroom, clicking the door to behind us.

"I bought him a bicycle as an early Christmas present," I told her. "Gave it to him, just now. Only it turns out he doesn't have the foggiest idea how to ride it. He just crashed straight to the ground."

Even as I offered it, I knew it sounded feeble. That in my panic I was—perversely—trying to give her back some ground.

"He fell off a bicycle? This is all because he fell off a bicycle?" She was incredulous.

"For Christ's sakes, Annie. No one in the history of the world has ever forgotten how to ride a bicycle!"

But the balance of probability had shifted in her favor and we both knew it.

She went to the window, where she stood looking out with her arms clamped about her as if attempting to contain the intensity of anger.

"I don't think you're well, Julian."

"The thing is, I've done a bit of research on amnesia, you see, and—"

She turned abruptly to face me, her eyes rounded in sorrow.

"I know about Francis Benson and that painting," she said. "He rang here the other day, not realizing you'd moved out. He sounded incredibly angry. He said you had made an unforgivable error and lost him a very substantial sum."

I had an odd sensation that the room was rushing towards me, and it was only the fortuitous proximity of the bedpost that saved me from stumbling.

"I mean, let's think about this, Julian. Just for a second." She spoke as if to a half-wit. "Are you seriously trying to suggest that a mother might not know her own son?" The scornful laugh that broke from her was so withering, the last bit of fight in me died. A silence fell between us, only the bass of the television booming up through the floor. If her sorrow had pained me, this cold contempt was far worse. Feeling nauseous and light-headed, I was about to sit down on the bed, but she gestured so regally to the door I turned instead and fled.

In the blink of an eye the world was slipping away from me. Just as if a dazzling light had come on so abruptly it had momentarily blinded me. She was right—it made no sense! I couldn't think what had possessed me. As soon as I got back to my flat I went to the bay window and wrested it open. The frame was covered in a grime that soiled my fingers, and a piercing wind entered the room, stirring the paperwork that was stacked in neat piles along the desk. I stood, taking in deep lungfuls of air.

From somewhere came the high wail of a baby, and glancing at the clock, I saw it was late now. The wisest thing would be to get an early night and review the matter in the morning. Instead, I fell to pacing. *For if this wasn't Dan, who in God's name was it? Where could he possibly have sprung from?* The baby was crying again. Or perhaps it had been there all along, like a low tinnitus. *How was a man to think clearly with such a racket going on?* I went out and hammered on my neighbor's door. It was some moments before it opened, the chain allowing just a narrow chink through which I could make out the bent figure of an elderly man.

"Could you *please* do something about that baby?" I cried, but he only offered a volley of angry abuse before stabbing a finger to his temple and slamming the door on me. At once the crying stopped.

I went back to my pacing. When all was said and done, it was this alleged state of amnesia that so obscured matters. Perhaps Dan gave the impression of being a stranger simply because he was no longer bound to any of us by a shared past? After all, what, if anything, remained of someone's identity, once memory had departed?

Eventually, I stopped my pacing to find the clock had inched to midnight. One last attempt, I bargained with myself. Forget this sophistry and abstraction and get to the nub of the matter. All I required was something in black and white to put before Annie in the morning. I went to the computer and switched it on. *An impostor has arrived in my family*, I typed with such speed I had to keep pausing to correct the letters—and up on the screen sprang something called *Capgras syndrome*: apparently a delusional disorder in which the sufferer becomes irrationally convinced that someone close to him has been replaced by an impostor. *People with this belief usually possess normal perceptions but are disturbed emotionally with paranoid tendencies.* I reread the entry several times, digesting this shocking new possibility before closing down the Internet and retiring to bed in turmoil.

Eventually, I drifted off to sleep, only to dream immediately and horribly. I dreamed that I was peering into the depths of the Lotto painting, with the dark staircase twisting through its center and the shadowed figures to left and right. I scanned it intently, keen to discern the marks of authenticity I had evidently overlooked at my first viewing. Yet what was Francis Benson talking about? Apart from anything else, the two figures were blatantly anachronistic. Puzzled, I leaned closer. Science-fiction heroes, if I wasn't much mistaken. I had always thought the shadowed man on the right was stoking a fire with a poker. Now I saw he was in actual fact holding some kind of laser gun. I was leaning closer still when he unexpectedly turned a blaze of searing light upon me, and before I knew it I was running down a never-ending flight of stairs sketched by Escher—and out into the windswept meadows.

I shouted out in terror. I had the impression I had woken—that I now rose from my bed, drawn by a rhythmic breathing. Someone was in my flat! It dawned on me with renewed horror that the boy had come for me. Not content with ousting me from Annie's house, he wanted to finish me off. Wasn't that the sound of his footsteps tiptoeing towards me through the darkened room?

I writhed this way and that, desperately trying to wake myself, until at last, I burst upwards out of sleep, the horror only receding as I took in the details of the room with the orange light from the street coming dimly through the curtains and everything quite still.

4

I set off for Annie's a little while before dawn, intending to wait outside until the household awakened. A fox ambled through the gates of a nearby garden, pausing for a while to regard me with cool indifference before resuming its lopsided trot and vanishing into the gardens opposite. The moment I saw the kitchen blinds open, I knocked on the door. When Annie answered, she was wrapped in her dressing gown, and the smell of bacon rose in a rich aroma on the wafts of warm air that came from the house. How dismal it felt to be savoring it this time from the doorstep. She frowned in irritation.

"Rachel's asleep."

"It's you I've come to see."

She didn't move.

"We need to talk."

Though she made no reply, I pressed on regardless.

"Are you absolutely certain?" I said.

"I'm absolutely certain."

Yet something about her, a wild light in her eyes, made me suspect she too had undergone a sleepless night.

"You don't think all this, this business of forgetting, strangely convenient?"

"Well, as you know, some memories are at last returning."

"Though so far nothing that can actually be verified."

"Oh, I see." She gave a harsh little laugh and glanced quickly towards the kitchen. "Let's see if we can remedy that then, shall we?"

She turned on her heel, leaving me to follow sheepishly in her wake. In the kitchen I found him at the table, shoveling down the remnants of a cooked breakfast. He offered a curt nod.

"What, you might well be asking yourself, could possibly have summoned Dan from his bed at such an hour?" she asked in a sardonic tone, gesturing for me to take the seat opposite him. "And the answer, of course, is Shania. Apparently, they have a hot date at the Queensway skating rink."

Then she clattered about filling the kettle while I sat stiff-backed, waiting.

Since Annie was too angry—seemingly with us both—to say any more, and he as usual appeared to feel no obligation to make any attempts at conversation, we sat in silence with only the quiet chatter of the radio and the sound of the kettle coming to a rolling boil. She set a cup in front of me, then the teapot, clunking them resentfully down before beginning to clear away his breakfast. He made not the slightest effort to help her. In the old days, Annie had always been strict about the children clearing up after themselves. It was one of the few domestic duties she had been punctilious in enforcing.

"I've got something to show you," she said to him in a studiedly off-hand tone as she bustled about. "When I was up in the loft yesterday, I found something I thought might amuse you."

She took up an album of photographs, polishing it with the sleeve of her dressing gown before setting it down before him. "Here. See what you make of this." He began to flick through, and after a moment, though she had started on the washing-up, she set the dishes aside and came to stand beside him, holding her wet hands in the air so that they dripped bubbles across the linoleum. Upside down, I could see various family groups smiling at the camera, and Rachel and Dan playing outside in what appeared to be a perpetual summer.

"Oh look," she laughed with pleasure, her voice softening despite herself. "Who's that then?" She was indicating a picture of a baby smiling winsomely into the camera.

"That's me, innit? And that," he indicated the white-haired man who held him, "that's Granddad."

She glanced at him, startled. "You remember!"

Her eyes flashed towards me so fleetingly it was almost subliminal. Dan stared at the picture for some time.

"And look at this one! Who do you think that is?" she asked in a reverent tone. He tore his eyes reluctantly from the baby and turned now to the picture she indicated.

"Dad!" he answered at once.

"That's right." Her eyes brimmed with tears. "Your dad."

"Before he got sick."

"Before he got sick." And again her eyes flew to me. *You see?* they flashed. *You see!*

"Check the hair," he said, indicating the youthful Annie who stood beside him—and they both laughed.

"Yes, all right, all right, you cheeky bugger! There's a lovely one of you on the next page, all covered in chicken pox." She jabbed him in the ribs, and he ducked away, snickering.

She went to dry her hands before drawing up a chair and sitting down beside him. After a moment they came to a large family group. He paused and ran a finger across the faces. "Granddad. Rach. Granny," he said in turn. "Think Dad must have been in hospital then."

She sat back in her chair, nodding several times.

"It's all there somewhere, isn't it!"

"Guess so," he said, looking faintly taken aback himself. "He was in hospital a lot, wasn't he? Never been able to stomach the smell of them since."

She reached out to touch his arm. "Do you remember how old you were when Dad died?"

He frowned. "About six, I think."

"Yes. Very young, you see. Far too young to really process it properly." How earnestly she addressed him. "And because you were so small, I'm ashamed to say I never gave you a proper chance to say good-bye. It was a mistake for which I owe you a very big apology. Not a day has passed in the last three years when I haven't had cause to regret it."

He was visibly discomforted, entwining his arms in a snaking motion, first one way, then the other, and noting this, she closed the book, assuming a magisterial air, as if she had now concluded the case for the defense. Then she fixed me with an expression of such imperious reproach, I took it as a dismissal and rose at once to my feet. But he sprang up too, wiping his mouth on his sleeve and muttering something about being late for Shania.

"But you haven't told me when you'll be back!" Annie called, hastening after him into the hall. I squeezed past them as they stood conferring, muttering my farewells, though they were too immersed to note my departure.

I found myself by the river stumbling along the muddy towpath. It was high tide, the ripe sweep of swollen water submerging the trunks of the willows along the banks. I had hoped the fresh air might clear my head, but the mud underfoot made progress hard. Was it possible that I was mistaken? That this *was* Dan, after all? I passed the dilapidated play park that lay beside the estate. Two teenage girls had climbed the rigging of the climbing frame, looking grotesquely incongruous as they dangled there. Both turned to watch me pass.

"Want some?" one of them called in a vulgar manner, hoicking her skirt up and thrusting a hip at me while her whey-faced companion cackled like a witch from behind her hand.

3

Finally, at a loss who else to turn to, I called Annie's sister, Emma. Now here I sat in the kitchen of her orderly North London home, waiting while she briefed the Polish laborer she was dispatching on a job. Since he spoke little English, the exchange between them was proving a laborious one, the edge of impatience that colored everything she said and did making the man visibly anxious. Emma was a landscape gardener, and as she had explained somewhat tersely when I called, this was a busy time of year for her. At last she resolved the matter to her satisfaction, and the man stepped away from her, nodding his head deferentially to demonstrate that his lack of understanding didn't indicate a lack of willingness.

"How's Jane?" I asked as she sat down opposite me, relieved that the question gave an impression of someone rather more in charge of his faculties than I felt myself to be.

"Oh, still fantasizing about jacking it all in. The latest idea is to buy an organic farm somewhere in the depths of Somerset."

We exchanged constrained smiles.

"So what is it that's so sensitive it can't be broached on the phone?"

"Well, I'm a bit worried about Annie. Or rather Dan. There are certain . . . oddities that have rattled me."

"Oddities?" She took an apple from the bowl and bit into it, nibbling in tiny reflective bites.

"Didn't you go and see her the other day?" I asked.

She nodded.

"And?"

"Well, I thought she was . . ." Emma made a gesture to indicate the inadequacy of language. "I thought she was happier than I had ever seen her. As you'd expect. I mean, I can't have been the only one who had given up hope. I feel terrible about that now. Not that I ever said anything. But when she called to say he had turned up again like that, I could hardly believe my ears! It was a bit like something out of a fairy story, wasn't it? So surreal and unexpected."

She spoke in a rush, her fingers raking through her hair. I scrutinized her with care.

"And what was your impression of Dan when you first saw him?"

She straightened and appeared to take a moment to restore a little distance between us before considering the question.

"My impression of him?" she repeated briskly. "Well, Dan's always been a bit of a dark horse, hasn't he? I've never really been able to make head nor tail of him. He seemed rather a . . . a lost soul, I suppose."

"Doesn't it strike you that the boy who went away is very different from the boy who has returned?"

She frowned. "Of course! I mean, he's gone through puberty for one thing. And I imagine that whatever has happened has deeply traumatized him. It doesn't really bear thinking about."

She bit her lip, seeming to weigh up whether to say more, before faltering into silence again. Eventually, she took out a packet of cigarettes, selecting one and lighting it thoughtfully.

"Look. I know what this is really about. I know exactly why you've come. Annie's sent you, hasn't she? You're probably under instructions to give me a bit of a ticking-off. And I know that I shouldn't have put the phone down on her like that, but as she probably told you, Jane and I have been having a few problems. And when she started lecturing me on relationships, I just thought it was bit rich really. Hello, kettle, and all that."

The doorbell rang, but she appeared not to hear it, reluctant to break her train of thought now she had embarked on it.

"She can be so bloody high-minded sometimes."

The bell rang again, and Emma hastened out of the room. When she returned, she was followed by the clown-faced Polish man bowed low beneath bags of compost. She sat down again.

"So here's the thing, Julian. Probably best to leave it well alone. Anyway, haven't you and Dan got a bit of bridge-building of your own to do? I seem to recall the two of you never exactly hit it off, did you?" She fixed me with a baleful stare. "I'd start by putting your own house in order, if I were you. After all, it's the only way you're ever going to get things back on track with Annie."

Then, glancing with a start at her watch, she sprang to her feet, cursing. "Oh, bollocks! Zak will be standing in the classroom door wondering where his mother is," she cried in dismay, stubbing out the cigarette and pulling on her coat. She gave a piercing whistle, and down the stairs came the eager feet of a dog who skidded alarmingly into the room, his claws clattering on the wooden floor. "Come on, you great stinking hound."

I followed them out to the street.

"Look—tell Annie I'll ring her, will you?" she called, as she loped off down the street at a half run, with the whippet prancing behind.

All the way home, the train's rhythmic clatter and roll amplified the confusion of thoughts that slid and collided within me. The encounter had only thrown me deeper into uncertainty. A mother, a sister, two schoolfriends, and now an aunt—who all appeared ready to accept this boy at face value. The memory of a colleague who had undergone some kind of breakdown came unexpectedly to me. A discreet phone call was all it would take to locate a psychiatrist who could assess me. Hadn't Annie once accused me of mistaking repression for self-control? But the point—*the point*—surely was this: *I had known from the outset.* Or rather it was as if two incompatible sound tracks had been running concurrently, and I had chosen to attend to the harmonies of one, while deliberately turning a deaf ear to the discord of the other.

In my professional life, long experience had taught me that when a work of art is authentic, everything hangs together. There are no oddities. If on closer inspection some aspect lets you down, its weaknesses will become only more manifest with every new viewing. On the other hand—already certainty was slipping away again—it was entirely possible that the exact opposite was true. That I had simply worked too long in a profession beset by duplicity, and in doing so, fatally skewed my perspective.

It was then that my eye was caught by the double-glazed window opposite. Mirrored in the imperceptibly vibrating glass, there appeared to be two distorted versions of me, their juddering faces superimposed upon each other, just like someone being violently shaken in two.

The days passed without further word from Annie, and it was Rachel who provided my only insight into the alarming turn of events now unfolding in the household. She confided that despite her mother's attempts to curtail him, Dan now spent most of his time out with Shania. On his return, the rows between Annie and Dan could be at times ferocious. We were sitting in Fitzi's Ice Cream Parlour, a favorite stop-off on the high street, while Rachel relayed this woeful state of affairs.

"He says that Mum's smothering him—that she's got to stop treating him like he was still a little kid." She was draining her bowl of every last trace of ice cream with a greedy finger. "He says she forces him to get out of the house just to get a bit of breathing space. Once Mum completely lost it and shouted that she wished he'd never come back! Afterwards she cried and said she couldn't believe she had ever said such a terrible thing."

Later that day, she said, the same reporter as before, this time accompanied by a photographer, had knocked on the door asking to interview Dan. He said they had it on good authority that Dan had been back for a while. In a way it was lucky Annie had just been crying. Did she look like a mother who was celebrating the return of her long-lost son? she had shouted at them. She said that if she ever saw either of them again, she would have them both arrested for harassment. Then she had slammed the door in their faces.

Rachel's eyes were wide with the drama of it all, but I kept my own counsel, only nodding ruminatively as I listened, turning it all over in my mind.

Later, after I dropped her off, I sat down and picked

up the phone, thinking I would try to trace the children's refuge in Glasgow. For it had occurred to me that if I could only speak to Luke Holland, he might be able to throw some new light on the matter. I made call after call. Hours passed, a morning slipped into an afternoon, and darkness fell. Yet I was unable to locate either a children's refuge or any careworker answering to that name. In fact, I could find no one in Glasgow able to substantiate a single aspect of Dan's story. Like a magician's rabbit, he'd apparently appeared out of thin air.

2

It was late that evening, as I was preparing for bed, when the phone rang. I knew immediately it must be Annie—and that her call at such an hour could only signal a crisis of some kind.

"I'm sorry to trouble you, Julian. I mean, I know it's nearly midnight," she said, her voice breaking, "but Dan hasn't come home—and I simply don't know who else to call."

Out on the street, I hailed a passing cab and arrived to find her sitting hunched at the kitchen table. It wrenched my heart to see her dear face so drawn, and it was some while before I could make any sense of the garbled story she offered. It seemed Dan had gone out with Shania earlier that evening, promising to be back by ten. So when ten o'clock had come and gone and there was no sign of him, Annie had rung his mobile, at first maddened by his failure to answer before she was seized by panic that history was repeating itself. Over and over his voice mail picked up until she knew every inflexion of his recorded voice exactly.

I took her phone from her, saying I would make one last attempt—and this time, to my surprise, Dan answered at once. The sound of live music was booming loudly in the background.

"What's up, Mummy dearest?" he asked, in a foolish singsong voice I had never heard before. When I demanded to know what the devil he thought he was playing at, he only guffawed, before assuming an accent I presumed was intended to parody my own.

"Well now, that, as they say, is the million-dollar question." His voice withdrew from the mouthpiece for a moment. "It's Jules—wanting to know *what the devil we think we're playing at.*" Somewhere in the background an officious voice began to instruct him to either move outside or switch the phone off, and an altercation appeared to break out between them. I heard Dan shouting angrily at the man to *fucking well back off*, before the line went abruptly silent.

I relayed all of this to Annie, and we took it in turns to keep dialing until eventually, after a dozen or so attempts, the phone was answered by someone with a broad Essex accent, sounding very angry indeed.

"Where is Dan?" I demanded in alarm.

"Who wants him?" the voice barked.

When I said I was a friend calling on behalf of Dan's mother, the voice emitted an aggrieved guffaw.

"Mother! Right. That figures. Only went and give me some cock-and-bull story about coming from a children's home, didn't he? Like I've got mug written all over me face." He gave a snort of indignation. "Well, anyone who wants him will find him at the police station." And with that, the line went dead again.

I tracked down the police station easily enough. The duty officer there explained that I must have spoken to the cab-driver who had brought Dan in after he had tried to flee his cab without paying. The driver had given chase and dragged him back to the vehicle before locking the doors and delivering him to the police station. They were going to wait for Dan to sober up overnight before deciding whether to charge him in the morning. In the commotion, he had left his phone on the backseat and the cabdriver had insisted on keeping it as security for the unpaid debt.

Annie took a deep breath when I relayed the news, clasping her head despondently in her hands.

"Well, at least we know where he is," she said in a dull tone. "And that he's safe."

When I went to collect him the following afternoon, he presented a woeful spectacle, sitting in the bleak reception area in his creased clothes with a black eye and an open cut across one cheek. He could barely meet my eye, and mumbled only the most reluctant of responses to my questions. It appeared that he and Shania had gone to a concert in

Shepherds Bush, where they'd both had too much to drink before getting thrown out by the bouncer. It was only on the way home in the cab that they realized neither of them had any money and decided to make a run for it.

"I know I've been a right wanker," he said morosely. "And if it makes you feel any better, I've never felt so rough in my entire life."

I nodded grimly. "Well, I can only say that you have no one to blame but yourself."

Earlier, the cabdriver had agreed not to press charges on condition he was fully reimbursed, and I had settled with him in full, before shaking hands and apologizing once again. His earlier rage had by now subsided. "I can see he comes from a decent enough family," he said, as he handed the phone back to me, "and to be perfectly honest, I feel sorry for you. I only hope for your sakes that the night in the cell might have knocked a bit of sense into the little bugger."

I told Dan that he would have to write a letter of apology, but he made no response, turning to look out of the car window as we crawled through the rush-hour traffic. Exasperated at what I took to be his indifference, I began to berate him. "Do you not think that Annie has been through enough already? She has taken you in with open arms, dedicating the past few weeks entirely to your welfare—and this is how you repay her. It is difficult to believe that a more thoughtless, *ungrateful* creature ever walked the earth."

He looked down at his lap. A shrug. An expression of abject misery. Then after a moment or two, I realized from the odd snuffling sounds he emitted that he was crying. I said nothing. Indeed, I was glad to see he might in actual fact have a conscience after all, and for the rest of the journey he continued to sit hunchbacked, sniveling wretchedly. It was a great relief to at last assert my authority. Evidently, the time to put my foot down was long overdue.

"You are not to contact Shania again," I told him, as we drew up outside Annie's house, "and you are now grounded for the remainder of the week."

He kept swiping the tears away with his sleeve, dabbing again and again at his running nose.

"Do you hear me?"

He nodded.

"So for the rest of the week you are . . . ?"

"Grounded." He spoke in the hoarsest of whispers.

The moment I parked the car, he fled into the house ahead of me and slammed up the stairs, leaving Annie to stand in the doorway of the kitchen looking after him with an expression almost as wretched as his own.

"I don't want to speak to him until I've had a chance to calm down," she said, sitting heavily on the nearest chair. "I honestly feel I'm at the end of my tether, Julian. For years I've been handing out breezy advice to the parents of my more wayward students—and now I find myself on the receiving end, I discover I'm just as much at a loss as anyone."

We kept the kitchen door closed, careful to speak in hushed voices, yet no sounds of life came from his room, and when I went to check on him, I saw from the dark strip beneath the door that he had switched the light off. I made Annie a simple supper before persuading her to take a bath and putting her to bed.

"Don't go," she whispered when I kissed her good night, her hand reaching out to pluck at my arm. She appeared so fragile as she lay curled beneath the covers that I climbed in beside her and held her, just as I had done so many times in the old days until she fell asleep in my arms.

I lay for some while listening to the rise and fall of her breath and the wind in the trees outside. Accept Dan or lose Annie. Only Emma would have put the case so bluntly. How straightforward the task of abiding by that advice would be, but for these puzzling and inconvenient doubts. Try as I might, I could neither silence the voice nor find a way past it. Once again the unanswerable questions rose in a swarm. *But if this wasn't Dan, who was it? Where in God's name might he have come from, and what was it he wanted?*

A gathering menace was thickening the darkness. I wondered about the wisdom of having spoken so harshly to him. Dangerous to kindle grievance in the breast of someone so mysterious, so potentially malign. What if I had precipitated him into action of some kind? Or retribution?

After a moment, I eased Annie out of my arms and went downstairs to get my BlackBerry. Her purse was lying on the table so I picked that up too. Then with something that felt part shame, part panic rising in my throat I sought out all the kitchen knives and put them away at the back of a cupboard. Halfway up the stairs, I came back on an afterthought for the car keys, carrying everything back to the bedroom and heaping it all on the floor beside me.

It was perhaps no more than an hour or so later that I snapped out of an uneasy doze. I had pulled myself upright before I worked out what it was that had awoken me—from somewhere in the house the insistent ring tones of a mobile phone. Moments later I heard his footsteps on the landing. I was on my feet at once, my heart hammering in my chest, waiting at the ready for the door to open. But the footsteps continued on past the bedroom, then a series of creaking stairs signaled a slow and furtive descent. I couldn't but curse him. This boy was becoming more troublesome by the hour. How incredibly stupid I had been not to have confiscated his phone.

I pulled on whatever clothes came to hand while Annie's breath rose and fell in peaceful repose. Perhaps the call had come from an accomplice waiting outside on the street. Between them they could probably strip what little there was of value in a matter of minutes. As I opened the bedroom door, I heard the front door quietly closing.

By the time I had flung on a coat, crammed my feet into shoes, and stepped from the house, the boy had already reached the end of the street, and it was with relief that I saw he was empty-handed. I was about to call his name when, rather than turning towards the main road, he turned sharply right towards the allotments and vanished from view. A fury grew in me that he should so boldly flout my authority in this way, and I set off at a trot, knowing how quickly he would be swallowed by the ink black of the unlit road that lay beyond.

There was no more than a thin sliver of moon to light my way, and as I drew level with the turning I saw him fleet momentarily ahead of me in the gloom before he vanished once more. Now that I could no longer see anything, my anger quickly gave way to fear again. It occurred to me that I could be walking into some kind of trap. That perhaps he had decided the only way to secure his position would be to dispatch me under cover of night. I did what I could to get a grip on myself, but by now I had lost any capacity to contain the animal fear that surged in me. It was as I drew level with the allotments, stumbling and rising over the speed bumps, that I caught what I took to be the rattle of the gate and the clink of a falling chain. Yet arriving at the gates only moments later, I found them securely locked. I stood in some confusion, with my face pressed to the wire mesh, until the sound of distant laughter startled me into life again and I set off with renewed determination, feeling my way along the boundary fence, hoping for a hidden entry of some kind.

On the far distant side, the Fishers Estate glowed brightly, the harshly lit courtyards more closely resembling a vast nocturnal prison camp than a block of residential flats. Only a fool would have left his bed to come stumbling blindly through these windswept fields, I thought, my fury now turning inwards. What in God's name was I doing out here?

Then, from somewhere close at hand, another whinny of laughter. Once more I hastened my step, catching my foot in the brambles and twice falling heavily against the fence. By now the noise was unmistakable, a heavy panting that caused the hairs on the back of my neck to rise unpleasantly. It was the movement that drew my eye, and peering through the tangle of branches, for the first time I could just make out their twisting forms. Two figures caught silhouetted in Mrs. Verdi's little shed, the sodium lights from the estate beyond making a vivid and shocking shadow play. A boy leaning over a reclining girl, thrusting against her with a jolting motion.

I fell back, my hands flying to my eyes as if I had received a bolt of electricity full in the face, stumbling once again and falling to my knees. But driven by the girl's moans as they rose in a sobbing crescendo, I regained my feet and retreated to the quietness of the unlit road beyond. A blessed silence returned as the distance between us grew, the only sensation now the jolt of tarmac beneath my feet and the violent agitation of blood through my veins. Back to the shadowy house, back to the sleeping Annie. Once in bed again, I lay rigid with adrenaline, my heart booming in the darkness. It was perhaps an hour later when I heard the soft click of the latch signal Dan's return. I thought it only too likely he would slip sweetly into a deep post-coital slumber, but I lay wide awake all that long, long night.

At breakfast Annie was subdued, setting the food down without a word, careful never to look in his direction, and

I found myself playing brusque intermediary, passing him the milk, asking him in return if he could hand the jam to Annie. Finally, he snatched up the last of the toast, cramming it into his mouth before wiping his mouth on his sleeve and springing to his feet. At once Annie's eyes flicked to me, as if imploring me to intervene.

"Where the devil do you think you're going?" I asked, though it appeared he hadn't heard me. Still Annie's eyes bore in upon me, as if she were the ventriloquist and I her mouthpiece. His hand was on the doorknob. I leaped to my feet, my chair falling backwards with a clatter.

"Now listen to me, young man. You know perfectly well you're grounded for the rest of the week."

This time he turned, a nervous energy animating him, like a wild creature preparing for flight, and offered a helpless shrug as if to suggest the matter was regretfully out of his hands. His eyes glittered black.

"I've people to see. Places to go."

He walked a step or two backwards through the door with an odd little smile that hovered somewhere between apology and defiance. Even in my peripheral vision I could see the apprehension of Annie's hunched posture.

"I'll see you when I see you, yeh?" he said, addressing her, and then he turned and was gone.

Annie folded forward in her chair, looking at once very old and tired. I walked to the dresser, as if drawn by an invisible thread, and picked up one of the photographs that cluttered the shelves. It was a school portrait of Dan aged about seven. I examined the smiling face for some moments. After a moment I began to laugh. It was ridiculous. Absurd! How willfully blind I had been. Dan's eyes in the picture were not dark at all. They were unmistakably blue.

"Annie, his eyes were blue and now they're brown."

She digested this for a moment before nodding gravely. "Yes, I know."

"You know!"

She barely seemed able to rouse herself. "Apparently there are drugs that can change the color of your eyes."

"Drugs that can change the color of your eyes!" I echoed, astonished at the calm authority with which she offered this.

"I looked it up—that first evening after he came home again. I can only imagine that someone at some stage must have given him something. Most probably without him even knowing."

"But why didn't you say something?"

"I tried to put it out of my mind. It was too awful to think about."

A long shrill note of astonishment rang in my ears. His eyes were blue and now they were brown. I put the picture down again, seeming to hear the click of a myriad small moments of uncertainty falling into place.

"So you still insist this is Dan?"

"Oh, don't start all that again, Julian," she sighed, passing a weary hand across her forehead.

"You do know that there is a way to settle this matter once and for all, don't you?"

At this her eyes fixed steadfastly on mine, and the silence in the house momentarily deepened.

"When Dan disappeared, the police filed some of his DNA. Do you remember? If you call them, it would be a perfectly straightforward matter for them to test him and make a comparison."

She half-laughed, shaking her head in disbelief, and though I took her hand in mine, she kept it tightly coiled in an unyielding fist. "Jesus, Julian. You just don't give up, do you?"

I waited for Annie in a café nearby, anxiously scanning the passersby. In the end she had been insistent she must deliver the "Judas kiss," as she called it, herself. And when Dan finally returned to Fishers Meadows later that afternoon, she had texted to tell me that they were now in the car on their way to the police station and asked that I give them an hour before meeting her here.

The café was strung with decorations that winked and blinked and sparkled, and from a tinny radio somewhere came the thin sound of a Christmas song. At last she appeared through the jostling shoppers, a little out of breath, looking more fragile and wan than I had ever seen her. She raised a tentative hand in greeting and came in to join me, clasping her coat tightly about her, carrying herself like someone with a difficult message to impart.

Dan had set off for the police station with surprisingly good grace. As we had agreed, she told him the blood test was just a formality the police required in order to close their file on him. It would be a relief to her, she had explained, not to live in a continual state of readiness for that knock at the door. But she had no sooner parked the car than he had completely lost his temper. *How dare she treat him like some kind of low-life criminal*! *Couldn't she see how cruel, how heartless it was to ask him to do such a thing after everything he had been through*? She had tried her best to soothe him, to assure him it was a mere technicality, but in truth she had been stricken with shame. He had stood with his back to her as she implored him to do whatever was necessary to allow them to resume a normal life again, before turning without a word and vanishing among the crowds.

"And you know something? He's right, really. He does deserve better. It was a relief, to tell you the truth. I can't pretend I wasn't dreading the prospect of having to deal with the police again."

That falling sensation in my belly again.

"I know you mean well, Julian, but we're fine as we are. Honestly. Maybe it doesn't all add up. I really don't know anymore." She gestured delicately, and only someone with a heart of stone could have remained unmoved by the anguish that fleeted across her face.

"But it is what it is." Her eyes roamed to and fro across my face. Then she touched my arm. "It's so close to Christmas now, you see . . ."

How ludicrous and yet poignant, I thought, a small glimmer of understanding dawning. For the past three years Christmas had been a time to be endured. She had looked on as scattered families regrouped. Did she really believe that if they could just reach Christmas, something about the rituals of the day would repair all discrepancies?

"I'd better dash," she said. "I promised the children they could decorate the cake."

She made a regretful gesture of farewell and turned for the door. The fact that it was over between us—the certain knowledge that it was the end—took my breath away. There were so many things I needed to say, even as the onset of leaden sadness made speech impossible. At the last moment, on a sudden impulse, she darted forward to offer a final kiss, and we bumped noses, before pulling away with mumbled apologies and foolish smiles.

1

The bitter wind carried it with the scent of ice. As I strode, it brought flurries of snow that grazed my cheeks. I passed the crooked forests of Christmas trees that had sprung up along the high street, their bright resin perfume bringing a sweet top note to the wind's passage. Five years of living in one place had been a mistake. All the unhappy times in my life occurred when I lingered too long. The thing that held you inevitably grew stale or ran dry. I thought fleetingly of Rachel, before wresting my mind into abeyance.

I found I was walking through the market, past the dismal shantytown shops that clustered beneath the railway arches, relieved to find the signs of seasonal festivity falling away. A group of Muslim women swathed in chadors were standing before the window of one of the shops, admiring the gaudy lengths of fabric displayed there. The signs were all in Arabic now. *There were no constants anymore. Only this restless, shifting flux.* I caught snatches of Hindi as I passed, fragments of Jamaican. Liberation lay in no one's hands but my own. I would simply slip away—no tears, or recriminations—no final showdowns. Best to take my chances overseas. How foolishly I had busied myself, building castles in the sky.

It was a while later that I lifted my head to find Fishers Meadows now opening up before me, with its great bowl of sky above, and the playing fields hunkered so low and squat below.

The house was unnaturally quiet when I let myself in—like a set waiting for family life to resume again. I knew from Rachel that the three of them would be out Christmas shopping all day. I looked about me for the last time. There was the dresser with its clutter of pictures and memorabilia. I noted the dead flowers in a jar on the table and the breakfast things yet to be cleared away. In the corner, a crooked Christmas tree awaiting decorations, beside it strings of tinsel in a heap on the floor. The usual piles of things teetered everywhere, even the new bicycle leaning against the wall was now festooned with shopping bags. If a room could represent the inner workings of a mind, then here was Annie laid out before me.

I put the keys on the table and muttered a quiet farewell. I suppose it was then it came to me. Or perhaps I had known all along. I had given myself the excuse of returning the key, but now I saw that my parting gift should be to end as I could have begun. Certainly I had nothing to lose anymore.

Taking one of the plastic bags that hung from the bicycle, I mounted the stairs two at a time. There, just as before, were the three toothbrushes lined up on the shelf in the bathroom. I picked up the boy's with care, using the plastic bag as a glove, before turning it neatly inside out and tying it with a bow.

It was the creak of the floorboard that startled me. Then the door swung open, and the boy's face appeared, reflected in the bathroom mirror above the sink. He was dressed only in pajama trousers, his eyes puffy from sleep and his hair still rumpled by the pillow.

"I thought you were going shopping?"

He shook his head. "Didn't fancy it."

We stood warily observing each other—something about the distance created by the reflection allowing this moment of candid scrutiny. The eyes so dark it was difficult to believe I had ever overlooked them.

"What are you doing?" He was peering at the toothbrush with curiosity, and I couldn't help but feel the absurdity of my situation.

"I'm on my way to the police station."

"The police station?"

"I think your deception has run its course, don't you?"

He appeared genuinely dumbfounded, taking a step backwards and folding his arms across his bare chest as if to defend himself.

"I don't understand."

As I set off down the stairs, his footsteps came close behind me.

"I said, I don't understand."

It took a few minutes to find Annie's car keys lying beneath a damp tea towel.

"As soon as it's established beyond reasonable doubt that you are not who you claim to be, the police will arrest you," I told him as matter-of-factly as I could. "No point in making a great song and dance about it." I opened the front door. "However, I would suggest you give some thought to what it is you intend to say to them once they get here."

"Please, Julian! Please . . . You're freaking me out," he cried, his face waxen.

I stepped into the street and wrenched open the car door, but in an instant he had run round to open the other side and thrown himself down beside me. A few heads were turning. I imagined the scene as it must appear to passersby, a bespectacled man brandishing a wrapped toothbrush, pursued by a boy in pajamas. I glimpsed Mrs. Verdi on her doorstep, with her hand paused midway to the door. So much for the tidy life she had ascribed us. A discarded coffee carton crunched underfoot.

"It makes no difference to me if you come or not." I slammed the door and put the key in the ignition. "You will simply be saving the police the trouble of having to come and find you."

I made a terrible hash of the gears, which gave out a protesting screech, pitching us first backwards and then forwards before we were at last on our way. He sat crouched in his seat, his eyes locked on the road while we passed the Fishers Estate, then, shortly afterwards, Fishers Comprehensive, crossing the lights as they went from amber to red as if propelled by a prevailing wind.

It was only a matter of minutes before we pulled up outside the police station. I switched off the engine and sat contemplating the glass doors. Was I really going to march in with the toothbrush and offer up my improbable tale? For a long while we sat in silence. I felt as a swimmer must whose every stroke bears him ever farther out of his depth. At length I roused myself and turned. He cut a wretched figure as he sat there, trembling with shock and cold, his bare chest and arms puckered by goose pimples.

"Okay. Here's the deal. I'll take you back—but only on condition you tell Annie everything."

He pursed his lips. Exhaled. Then shifted uneasily, flashing the whites of his eyes towards me in a brief surreptitious assessment.

"Just cut the amnesia crap. A few basic facts. That's all I'm asking."

He sighed, then jerked his head. Without another word I switched the engine on again and turned the car for home.

We came to a gentle halt outside the house.

"She'll be home very shortly. Perhaps you'd better go and find something warm to put on."

Clasping himself in a vain attempt to still the spasms of shivering, he got out, his teeth audibly chattering.

"Here." I wound the window down and held out his toothbrush. "You'll be needing this."

Over his shoulder I saw that a handful of journalists were now clustered outside Barbara's house with notebooks and microphones at the ready, while Barbara herself stood before them with her arms folded in defiance.

"Gentlemen. Like I told the reporter that come the other day, I'm saying nothing. My lips are sealed."

Dan snatched the toothbrush from me and turned to scuttle up the path to the house. But catching sight of him, one of the journalists cried out, and at once they all turned and ran in a straggling pack towards him. He was some way ahead though and reached the house just in time, the door slamming behind him.

As I watched from the safety of the car, they all congregated about Annie's gate, exactly as they had done three years before. Most had their phones clamped to their ear now and were issuing urgent instructions. A van bearing the Sky News logo, with a satellite dish on top, turned into the close and pulled up beside them. Two of the journalists came over to confer with the driver. From the comic gestures they made, they appeared to be reenacting Dan's bolt for the house. All three looked over at Annie's house, scanning the windows, then the driver checked his watch and sat scratching his chin in a ruminative fashion.

I sat at the wheel watching the planes as they dipped

down towards Heathrow through the red haze of the setting sun. I recalled Annie's description when she met him at the train station. *He looked so alone and afraid,* she had told me. Was it in that moment she had known yet simultaneously decided to put the knowledge from her? What was that curious phrase she had used? *It is what it is.*

I sat while the streetlamps clicked on one by one along the darkening road. Commuters were returning home, listening to headphones as they strode, glancing with idle curiosity towards the huddled group of journalists. A woman paused beside me, staring into space while her dog peed against a lamppost. Behind closed doors people were settling down in front of their televisions, the pressures of the day receding.

Still I sat. At length, Annie and Rachel appeared at the top of the street. They were walking slowly, bowed by heavy bags of Christmas shopping—and apprehension went through me like a blade.

I got out of the car and leaned against it, waiting as Annie drew nearer. She was so deep in contemplation, I thought for a moment she might pass blindly by, but I uttered her name and she turned quickly in my direction.

"What are you doing out here in the freezing cold?" she asked.

"I'm afraid a few journalists and photographers have begun to gather outside your house," I said, as I bent to take the heavy bags from her, falling into step beside them. "Thought you could probably do with some moral support."

"Oh Christ."

We turned the corner of the close, and Annie paused for a moment, surveying them in dismay. "Well, I can't say I'm surprised. We always knew it was only a matter of time, didn't we?" She began hunting for the door keys in her bag, preparing herself. "Is he home, do you know?" she asked anxiously.

I nodded, and she linked her arm through mine, as if for courage as we set off towards the journalists, bearing Rachel briskly before us. As we came abreast of them we put our heads down and pushed our way through, ignoring the jabbing microphones and bombardment of impertinent questions. "*Mrs. Wray, Mrs. Wray, is it true your son has come home again?*" "*Little girl, can I just ask you what you felt when your brother . . .*" "*On behalf of our readers, I wonder if you can describe . . .*" Then we were through, and the door had closed behind us.

Annie leaned against the door, tipping her head back and closing her eyes. "Vultures!" she said with a shudder. The phone was ringing. No sooner had it stopped than it began again.

"I imagine it won't be long now." She was looking into the sitting room with a frown, pondering something.

"Before the police come?"

She nodded. Then she went to the foot of the stairs, hissing, so that the press outside might not hear her. "Dan!" Only silence. She hissed his name again. Still nothing stirred. At once Rachel ran up the stairs ahead of her, softly calling his name again.

"I have to go away on business," I said. But Annie was looking about her distractedly. "In fact, the likelihood is that I will be gone for some time," I went on, aware I was speaking to no one.

"Why on earth is the house so cold?"

Craning her head this way and that, Annie followed the drafts of fresh air and disappeared into the kitchen. Then, "Oh!" I heard her exclaim. "Oh!" she said again, as I hastened to join her.

The back door stood ajar. Already a few autumn leaves had blown in.

"*Dan!*" she exclaimed sharply, yet without any apparent expectation of an answer. She turned towards me, scanning my face for an explanation, blinking slowly like someone awakening from a dream.

"I see," she said. Her eyes were rounded with a wonderment that was almost childlike in its sorrow.

Then after a moment she stretched out her hand and stepped towards the door. Perhaps it was only appropriate he should have left this last gesture to her, I thought, looking on. As I turned to go, I heard the soft click of the key and then the bolt go home.

Epilogue

In one hand I hold her card, on the front the painting by Constable with its dainty cloudscape, in the other the little news cutting which I now, reluctantly, unfold. I can't deny that her card, together with the rush of memories it has provoked, has left me somewhat shaky. In some closed compartment I have stored the whole affair as an unsolved mystery, a ghost story.

When I smooth the cutting flat it is the headline that leaps to the eye. CON BOY UNMASKED. A boy claiming to be an orphan on the run from gang warfare had been taken in by a kindly Nottingham clergyman and his wife, before being unmasked as a fraud and dubbed the Chameleon by the British press. The boy's name was Peter Braden, and the police discovered that, despite being semiliterate, over the years he had used the Internet to create a series of identities as an abused or abandoned child, sometimes imaginary but more often real, with the sole intention of persuading unwitting families to take him under their wing.

He had displayed a remarkable cunning, together with a prodigious imagination, on one occasion posing as an exploited itinerant circus performer and on another as the displaced son of Bosnian refugees tragically killed in the civil war. The police suspected that there were many other families who had been taken in and asked that anyone implicated come forward to identify themselves.

Braden was now on bail, awaiting charges of deception. Much was made of his early abandonment by his mother and a childhood spent moving between various residential homes and foster care. The headmistress of the school in which the clergyman had enrolled him described the boy as astonishingly plausible, while the arresting officer said that he had never come across a crime quite like it. "Usually people set up scams for money, but this boy's profit appears to have been purely emotional."

I read the article twice more before putting it away and setting off along the beach. The fine evening has attracted a lovely display of gaily colored sailing boats that dance in every direction across the glittering sea. Could this really be the same boy who had appeared to such devastating effect in our lives? Presumably, Annie was sending me the article because she thought it at the very least a possibility. And I suppose that it could indeed be the explanation I have craved all this while. Certainly there are no obvious incompatibilities of detail with which I can definitively rule it out.

And yet. And yet. Despite my best efforts not to dwell on it, there is another explanation that haunts me. One I was reminded of only the other day when I heard that the current owner of the Lorenzo Lotto painting had made an application for an export license and that it was now valued at a record-breaking five million. Somewhere far away on Bond Street, I knew that Francis Benson would be roundly cursing me again. A one-off blunder on my part? Perhaps. Yet the plain truth of the matter is this. In a court of law, the defending lawyer would have given my clinching evidence—the fact that the boy's eyes had changed color—short shrift. My subsequent research soon established that there are indeed certain drugs capable of changing eye color from blue to brown, after all. As time moved on, this discovery brought about an inexorable disintegration of confidence in the open-and-shut case I had constructed for myself. The discrepancies that had appeared so compelling began to strike me as potentially no more than tricks of the light generated by an undoubtedly fragile state of mind. The implications, as I say, have proved difficult to shake.

In the years since I have lived in California, I have led an uneventful life. Upon arrival, I spent some time in a clinic. All water under the bridge now. But when I came out I found the loss of trust in my judgment meant it was no longer possible to pursue my old profession. I moved sideways into restoration, where I have met with modest success.

There have been no significant relationships. I have kept my head down. At times I have even known something akin to contentment, when the wind was in the right direction.

It is sobering to reflect that such a considerable period could have elapsed without a word between us. Dan would have been twenty-five this year, while his sister, at twenty-one, has come of age. Annie remains the one—indeed the only—great love of my life. But I am not a sentimental man—it is a chapter that is closed now. I will go about my business and little by little put it all from me once more.

This novel is dedicated to the boy whose story inspired it, Nicholas Barclay, who disappeared in 1994 at the age of twelve and whose fate remains unknown.

In 1998, Frédéric Bourdin, the serial imposter who stole his identity, was imprisoned for six years.

Deceptions

REBECCA FRAYN

A Readers Club Guide

Introduction

Julian and Annie have just announced their upcoming marriage, when the unthinkable occurs—Annie's son, Dan, disappears on his way home from school. An intense search is conducted, but Dan has vanished. Determined to remain optimistic, Annie sees her son's face everywhere she goes, and she tells her younger daughter, Rachel, that her brother has simply gone away on a long trip. As the weeks turn into months, and months into years, Julian urges Annie to move on, longing for the woman he once knew and loved. But Annie refuses to give up hope. Three years later, her faith seems to pay off when Dan reappears. As the family adapts to the return of their son and brother, who is now a stranger, Julian can't ignore the doubts festering in his mind, causing him to question everything he thinks he knows.

Questions and Topics for Discussion

1. At the beginning of the novel, Annie proclaims, "We're just a perfectly average happy family, aren't we?" (p. 19) Do Julian's early experiences with Annie and her kids contradict this? Do you think the family is "average" in any way?
2. Annie insists to the police that Dan would never run away from home. What do we know about her family that could make this idea a possibility?
3. Discuss the early days of Julian and Annie's relationship. What attracts them to each other? How do the initial conflicts between them foreshadow the later problems they'll face in their relationship?
4. How much does Annie's grief over losing her husband contribute to her behavior? How does his death influence the other characters?
5. A major concern for Annie is which school Dan should attend. When she decides to send him to the local school, Julian disagrees with her. What does this incident reveal regarding Annie's ideas about raising her son?
6. On page 41, Julian thinks, "In time, everything became tainted by what she grew to think of as our fundamental differences in ideology." What is he saying here? How does Annie and Julian's perception of each other affect their relationship?
7. At his new school Dan began to change in a way that

was alarming to his mother and Julian. Do you think this should have been cause for concern, in the way that Julian and Annie saw it, or was his behavior typical of a teenager?

8. When Dan disappears, Julian is racked by guilt at his own failure to connect with the boy, and this feeling is partly reinforced by Annie. Should Julian feel guilty?
9. As Dan's absence continues, Julian notices that Annie slips into "the comfort of a narrative" (p. 88). What do you think he means? How is Annie using this narrative to cope with the loss of her son?
10. Discuss how Annie treats her daughter, Rachel, after Dan disappears. Do you think Annie should have lied to Rachel about Dan's absence? What would you have done differently if you were in Annie's situation?
11. On page 116, Annie and Julian have an argument that results in Annie kicking Julian out of the house. What finally pushes her to end their relationship? Do you sympathize with her decision?
12. When Dan returns, Annie defies reason and refuses to inform the police or allow visitors to the house. Why does she do this? How much do you think Annie understands about the situation?
13. What makes Julian suspicious about Dan when he returns? Why does it take him so long to act on these suspicions?
14. Throughout the novel, the only perspective the reader

has is Julian's. How does Julian's narration affect how we view the story? What do you think we don't see?

15. There are many layers of deception in this story, and the title itself is *Deceptions*. Who is the most deceived here? Are Julian's doubts somehow more compelling than Annie's unwavering faith?
16. What conclusions, if any, can we draw from this story about what we perceive and what we judge to be true? How do our own desires cloud our judgment?

Enhance Your Book Club

1. Learn more about the story of Nicholas Barclay and Frédéric Bourdin. Discuss how Bourdin was so successful and what motivated him to deceive so many people. You can find a profile of Bourdin at www.newyorker.com/reporting/2008/08/11/080811fa_fact_grann.
2. Annie explains the strange behavior of "Dan" by saying he has dissociative fugue, and Julian later thinks he has Capgras syndrome. You can learn more about these conditions by visiting the following websites: http://en.wikipedia.org/wiki/Capgras_delusion and www.merck.com/mmhe/sec07/ch106/ch106d.html. Discuss if these conditions could apply to any other famous characters in literature.
3. Julian works as an art appraiser, identifying forgeries for potential buyers. Read about the world of art forgery and about some of the more famous hoaxes in history at http://en.wikipedia.org/wiki/Art_forgery. Watch the movie *The Thomas Crown Affair*, which features an art heist and an expert forger.
4. Learn more about Rebecca Frayn and her work by visiting her website at www.rebeccafrayn.co.uk.

A Conversation with Rebecca Frayn

You dedicate the novel and the inspiration for Dan's story to Nicholas Barclay. What fascinated you about his story, and that of his imposter, Frédéric Bourdin?

I was reading the newspaper one idle Saturday afternoon when I came across an article which held me spellbound from beginning to end. It told such a compelling tale of an American family and the bizarre deception that had unfolded within it that afterwards I couldn't get it out of my head. Self-deception—the way in which we can know something yet keep that knowledge from ourselves—is something that has always fascinated me. And here was one of the most remarkable examples of self-deception I had ever come across. This combined with the fascinating psychology of Frédéric Bourdin, a serial fantasist in search of a family, seemed quite irresistible. So one day I sat down and, taking the barest bones of the real story, embarked on a psychological thriller about Annie Wray and what happens when her twelve-year-old son, Dan, goes missing.

Annie is a complex character, fiercely devoted to her family but often irrational in her decisions. How much of your own experiences as a mother went in to creating the multifaceted portrayal of Annie?

I'm a mother of three children, the eldest of whom are twin boys, Jack and Finn. And their age exactly paralleled the age of the missing boy as I wrote. Dan Wray is twelve when he goes missing—the same age as my sons when I began—and fifteen when he returns, as were my sons by the time I completed the novel. So inevitably I drew on the intense wellspring of feeling that I—like all mothers—feel for their children. But Annie is definitely not a portrait of me: her inconsistencies are uniquely her own.

One of the big debates Julian and Annie have is about where Dan should go to school. Can you fill in your American readers about the basic issues at stake and explain what makes English schools different from American ones?

Ever since I was a child, the choice between state comprehensive schools (non–fee paying schools open to everyone) and private schools (fee paying and only open to the minority who can afford them) has aroused much heated debate. Though 90 percent of children in England attend state school (as Dan does), the privileged private school graduates form an elite who continue to monopolize the top colleges and jobs.

Most private schools are for day pupils, but there are a number of private boarding schools, to which children may be sent as early as age seven and where they will remain until they're eighteen. It was the traditional way the upper classes broke the allegiance of their sons to the family and prepared them to go out and run the British colonies.

The narrator, Julian Poulter, has been educated at Harrow, a boarding school founded in 1572, where the students still to this day wear tailcoat and striped trousers on Sundays. Although his experience is only obliquely alluded to in the novel, his being raised in an institution from such a young age is absolutely key to understanding Julian's buttoned-up character. Many—perhaps most—of the British men I know were educated in this way and are probably fairly equally divided between those that loved the experience and those that (like my husband) loathed it. My own education was more akin to Annie's. Because of my parent's politics—they believed in an equal education for all—I was educated at local London state schools from the age of five to eighteen.

Did you go through a similar debate when it came to your own children?

When it came to my own children, I was very conflicted on the issue. Like Annie, I believe that state schools offer a more egalitarian and socially diverse experience. Our local state primary school is small and very good, so that's where my children were educated until the age of 11. But our local secondary school is huge and beset by complex social issues very like those of Fishers Comprehensive in the novel. So once my children reached eleven, we sent them to a nearby private school. Boarding school was never an option that either my husband or I ever considered.

Rachel becomes somewhat the forgotten child as the story goes on. If you could imagine her as an adult, what would

she be like, and how do you think she would be affected by what happened to her family when she was young?

It makes my heart twist to consider the long-term consequences for Rachel. I can only assume that such a disturbing experience would run very deep and have lasting consequences. This is a girl who grew up in a house where nothing is what it seems and people are not entirely straight with you about what is going on. A sibling might disappear, return, then vanish again. I would imagine that Rachel as an adult will have trouble establishing relationships and trusting in their continuity.

Which character did you enjoy writing the most?

When I began writing the novel, I didn't much care for the narrator, Julian Poulter. He holds so many views that are diametrically opposed to my own, and if I met him at a dinner party, I would find him too pompous and emotionally repressed. But it turned out to be very liberating writing from his point of view for precisely those reasons: he offered me a new perspective on all kinds of issues and made me challenge many of my long-held assumptions. Julian believes it's important not to delve into painful emotions, for example, whereas I had always believed that happiness comes through an honest engagement with our hidden selves. And I came to see him in many ways as a victim of his boarding school education. In time, to my surprise, I grew genuinely fond of him, and when the book was finished found I rather missed him.

Did you always know you wanted to write the novel from Julian's perspective? Did that decision hinder or help you in telling this story?

From the outset I felt the story would be more intriguing if I could tell it at one step removed. I wanted the reader to have to peer over the shoulder of a narrator who had a vested interest in establishing the truth yet is continually kept at arm's length for the unfolding action. Though Julian is the reader's filter for everything that unfolds, it gradually becomes apparent that his own agenda is almost certainly corrupting his interpretation of events. We learn that he is emotionally repressed, that he has in many ways resented Dan; yet he is so sexually and romantically obsessed with Annie that he is ultimately ready to try to will himself into a state of myopia about what is occurring. All of which helps to add a sinister uncertainty to the story and means the reader is hopefully tantalized by having to try to discern not only what is actually going on but also exactly how much to trust Julian's interpretation of the events as they unfold.

Your first novel was also about a family in crisis. What interests you about these situations and why do they make for good reading?

I grew up in a home that was fairly stable until I became a teenager, when our family circumstances changed quite abruptly and life became very turbulent. The effects of this were far-reaching and have taken some time and determination to unravel. But I am struck by how common this experience is, by how many of us—perhaps most of us—in different ways, at different times have endured periods when the home environment in which we hoped to be protected and nurtured becomes instead a place of turbulence and distress. For me there is catharsis in stories which delicately unpack crisis—and comfort to be derived from recognizing how universal this experience of conflict is. And I think it's also reassuring to be reminded of the way in which people can and do ultimately survive.

In addition to writing novels, you are also a critically acclaimed filmmaker. How is the process of writing different from making films?

I had directed lots of documentaries and drama before I signed a two-book deal with Simon & Schuster; and the move from filmmaking to novel writing was initially something of a shock, since I had always worked closely with a tightly knit team and actively relished the creative camaraderie. It took time to adjust to the intense isolation of sitting alone for weeks that became months and ultimately years—and to a process that is at times dangerously close to schizophrenia: an intense ongoing conversation with yourself.

The other early surprise was an unexpected attack of indecisiveness. As a filmmaker I was often frustrated by people's reluctance to talk publicly about the most interesting aspects of their story. Not to mention constrained by the restrictions of budget and logistics that always limited what you were actually able to achieve. But it was only once these restrictions were lifted that I realized how difficult it is to make a decision once *anything* is possible. In a novel my characters could have a sex change, sprout wings and circle twice round the world, and no one was going to tell me it wasn't possible. Rather to my surprise, I found my fingers lingering uncertainly over the keyboard, the options suddenly so overwhelming, I couldn't quite think how to begin.

Can you tell us a little about your next novel?

In the scorching temperatures of an August heat wave, three generations of the Bower family gather in Ibiza for a lavish party to celebrate banker William's fiftieth birthday on his newly completed luxury estate. He hopes the celebration can help forge some kind of reconciliation with his estranged daughter, Alice. But as a newly committed environmental campaigner, she turns out to be horrified by what she sees as his assault on the diminishing resources of the island. This novel will explore fragmenting family bonds and the fragile future of our planet.